SHUNNED

SEAL Team: Disavowed - Book Three

LAURA MARIE
ALTOM

Shunned
Copyright © 2016 Laura Marie Altom

SEAL Team: Disavowed series

To become a United States Navy SEAL, a man must be physically forged in steel and able to mentally compute life or death situations with laser accuracy and speed. Our country trusts these men with the most sensitive military operations—many so covert that once they are successfully completed, they are never spoken of again.

This series celebrates one particularly fierce band of brothers who valiantly battled terrorists whose crimes against nature and humanity were far too great to chance escape. On a dark night, on foreign soil, SEAL Team Alpha witnessed acts so unspeakably cruel against women, infants and small children that their consciences would not allow anything other than their own brand of justice for the scum terrorist cell.

A trial would have been too good for these pigs, and so, one-by-one they were taken out, and the women and children they'd used were freed. By dawn, an entire region breathed easier. The men of Alpha found themselves heroes to those whose lives they had saved, but virtual criminals in the eyes of the organization they served. After a lengthy investigation, their elite, covert team was formally disbanded.

They now spend their lives deep undercover, still serving—no longer their country, but individuals who find themselves in need of not only their own personal warrior, but a particular brand of justice.

While honorably discharged, these men and their actions will forever be *disavowed* . . .

SEAL Team: Disavowed series

1

Piapoco, Colombia

The baby was a fake.

Disavowed Navy SEAL Everett Black snatched the doll out of the crib by its shaggy black hair, pitching it across the dark room where it fell with a thump atop thick carpet. What was he going to tell Nash and Maisey? They'd trusted him to come to Colombia. To break into the heavily guarded compound of Vicente Rodriguez's widow and take back their kidnapped son.

What now?

Pulse revved, he darted his gaze about the typical nursery. Crib. Changing table. Rocking chair. What was he missing? Was this whole scene a set-up? Had the infant ever been in the freaking castle this chick called home? Or was the intel Trident, Inc. had been given misinformation? Meaning the Widow Rodriguez had been one step ahead of them since the baby had been snatched twenty-four hours earlier.

Gauzy curtains floated in the light breeze.

Time for him to fly.

He'd report his findings to Nash and the rest of the team, then lay low until receiving further instructions.

After sticking the decoy baby back in the crib to hopefully hide the fact that he'd ever been there, Everett pushed aside the curtains, straddling the windowsill.

Since free climbing was kinda his thing, it was no biggie to maneuver himself sideways onto the third floor ledge, then use the limestone mansion's elaborate sills and moldings for handholds. Earlier, he'd run a dummy signal through the security system, making it feel nice and cozy the whole time he'd been breaking and entering. He'd remotely switch it back once he got clear.

Everett reached the second-floor ballroom's balcony when a metallic click caught his attention. He froze.

He hadn't worn NVGs, partly because the moon was nearly full and he didn't figure he'd need them. Mostly, because he'd been afraid Baby Joe would have taken one look at "Uncle Everett" in scary monster glasses and freaked. Now, he wished he had them so he could make out the source of the noise.

Only when he heard muffled voices did he start to sweat.

June in Colombia was no joke, but up until now, adrenaline had kept him cool. There hadn't been time to do a thorough study of guard activity, but intel said there were always three rotating crews of security teams. Two guards monitored the house, and six watched the grounds. Thus far, they'd done a piss-poor job, considering he had yet to see one.

Odds were in his favor that the noise he'd heard had been one of the regular patrols making rounds.

When he didn't hear another sound save for a gazillion bugs' rhythmic humming, he figured he was free to scale the last floor, then hightail it through the mountainous jungle to the Jeep he'd stashed a few miles from the compound.

Antsy to make a quick exit, Everett braced his palms on the balcony's stone rail, then vaulted himself over.

At that instant, a blinding beam spotlighted him.

"*¡Al ladrón!*"

Translation? *Shit*.

He grabbed for the next handhold just as shots were fired. One pinged close enough for him to see sparks.

Pulse racing, he sucked in a deep breath and hoped for the best as he reached blindly for his next perch. What he got was a freefall, a seriously not good twist to his left knee, then, when he tried standing on it, he fell ass-backwards onto the manicured lawn.

He tried hopping up, but screaming pain sent him crashing back down.

Adding to the party were a circle of at least a dozen seriously armed commando-types holding M16s. All headlamps aimed at him.

He groaned. Why had he made this a solo mission?

"What a wonderful surprise," a smoky female voice said with a thick Spanish accent.

The lights being shone in Everett's eyes made it too bright to see the woman attached to the voice. The lady of the house?

"I do love a party," she said. "Although next time, please call first." He still couldn't see her, but her perfume was cloying—choking him with the crisp floral scent of high maintenance. "Take him away. See that he has medical attention for his knee. He could possibly make a nice trade for that bitch who killed my husband."

2

Sister Mary Margaret O'Hanlon fidgeted in the straight-backed chair, wiping her sweaty palms on her habit's long, gray skirt. This was it. After five years of waiting to finally become a full member of Our Mother of the Blessed Angel, she had been called into Mother Superior's office to be given the happy news that she was soon to undergo the final ceremony that would mark her permanent acceptance into the convent.

The room smelled of Vicks VapoRub and the lemon oil Sister Helen used to clean the convent's miles of wood trim.

"Ah, I should have known you'd be early."

Proving how much she'd learned, though Mary Margaret's natural inclination would be to grin, she tamped down her joy. Rather than sporting a giddy smile, she slowly exhaled, nodding while forcing her lips into a prim line. "Did you and the senior sisters meet?"

"We did."

Heart pounding loud enough for her to hear it in her ears, while Sister Agnes sat behind her imposing oak desk, Mary scooted to the front of her chair. *And?* She longed to blurt the question, but didn't. More modern convents encouraged sharing of feelings through conversation, but Our Blessed Mother followed a strict, traditional set of rules, both in behavior and dress. During the day, the sisters worked in the small local hospital and orphanage founded by their most generous benefactors, Camilla and Vicente Rodriguez. By night, after evening prayers, silence was required in order to foster deeper spiritual reflection. There were no mirrors and beyond general cleanliness, personal grooming was discouraged.

Sister Agnes leaned forward, clasping her hands atop her desk.

When she sighed, Mary Margaret's heart sank. She'd been through this too many times not to know what came next.

"Dear Sister, you know we love you and appreciate all that you do, but please understand that you came to us as a young girl who never—"

"No!" Mary Margaret shocked even herself by

slapping her palms atop the imposing desk. "I'm tired of hearing that just because I've never been anywhere else, that I'm somehow different. I don't want to go anywhere else. This is my home. You and the other sisters . . ." Her voice cracked. "You are my family."

"Child . . ." Sister Agnes left her chair to enfold Mary Margaret in a hug. "Please try to understand this decision wasn't easy—for any of us. We love you. You are a bright spot in all of our days. But when authorities brought you to us after you having lost your parents, we expected you to return to America as soon as family arrived. When they didn't . . ." She stepped back to shrug. "Yes, we became your family. But that doesn't mean you're meant to spend your entire life in the order. You're so young." She tidied Mary Margaret's eternally askew wimple and black veil. "Taking your final vows is a serious matter. Tonight, during your prayers, look inward, my child. Ask yourself if you truly desire to spend your life in the service of God, or if you are merely here because you feel you have nowhere else to go."

Everett woke to a dry mouth that tasted like wallpaper paste.

His eyes took forever to focus.

His head throbbed like he'd been on a two-day bender, but then the events of the previous night rushed back. Had the black widow drugged him?

He sat up in a narrow, hospital-type bed, raising his hand for a morning scratch, only to find both wrists cuffed to the bed's metal rails. This ordinarily wouldn't have been an issue, as he kept modified bobby pins in both side pockets of his cargo pants, but while he'd been out, Everett had been stripped of all of his gear and clothing and now wore a standard-issue pale green hospital gown.

He scanned the room.

Whitewashed stone walls. A tall, thin stained glass window not wide enough for him to squeeze through. A nightstand holding a lamp and Bible. A rolling metal tray loaded with a sweating, stainless steel water pitcher and an empty glass. A closed door faced him, as did a picture of smiling Jesus with his arms outstretched to a gathering of children.

"When you get a sec," he mumbled to the painting, "I could use a hand."

As if on cue, the door swung open.

An angel entered.

Holy shit. Everett was pretty sure it broke all kinds of rules to find a nun attractive, but this one had big blue eyes, full, kissable lips and a complexion so creamy she appeared to be made of porcelain. He closed his eyes for a sec to ensure he wasn't hallucinating, but sure enough, she was still there and still hot. Even better—bobby pins held her nun hat in place. All he needed was one to pick his cuffs, then get the hell out of Dodge.

She froze with her hand on the old-fashioned brass doorknob. Where was he? In the black widow's charity hospital? She had balls.

"You're awake," his angel said in perfect English with what he could have sworn held a hint of a deep Texas accent.

"You're American?"

She nodded, approaching with a blood pressure cuff. A stethoscope hung like a necklace around her white-collared throat. "My parents were missionaries. We moved to Columbia when I was in sixth grade." She wrapped her small, nimble fingers around his bicep, fitting the blood pressure cuff. Had his resulting bolt of awareness been due to an actual attraction to a nun or the drugs? He opted for the drugs. He'd done some crazy shit in his days, but getting attached to a woman who was already married to God wasn't his thing.

Still . . . That didn't mean he couldn't sweet talk her for information—or even secure unwitting help in making a quick escape.

Her eyes widened while studying the cuffs trapping him in the bed. He took that to mean handcuffed patients weren't all that common.

Interesting. What the hell kind of game was Camilla Rodriguez playing?

Everett cleared his throat. "You mentioned your parents were missionaries. What are they doing now?"

She froze. For an awkward few seconds, their gazes locked. It was too damned long, but not nearly long enough. "Unless the local cemetery suffered a natural disaster that failed to make the news, I would imagine they're both still in their graves."

Ouch. Wrong approach. "Sorry. I didn't know."

"Of course. How could you?" Was it his imagination, or was she pumping the cuff too damned full? When he winced, she let off the pressure, pressing the business-end of her stethoscope against his inner elbow.

"My folks passed when I was ten. How old were you?" The lie stung. But he needed a conversational ice breaker. If he were to have any chance of getting out of here, befriending the nun could be key. Thankfully, Doris and Fred were as active as ever in their Boca Raton retirement condo.

"Twelve. I'm sorry for your loss, as well." Yahtzee. Her tone had softened.

"What happened? Mine died in a car wreck."

Tears shone in her eyes. He was an ass. *I'm sorry*, his conscience said when his mouth couldn't. "They were trying to locate an orphaned child's grandparents when what they thought was a village turned out to be a drug smuggler's encampment.

They were both shot on sight."

Christ . . . "You witnessed this?"

She noted his blood pressure on a chart, then shook her head. "Thankfully, I was in school that afternoon. But if I hadn't been, I assume I would also be dead. Word travels fast. When family back in Texas delivered one excuse after another for why they couldn't come get me, Sister Agnes took me in, and I never looked back. The church is my only way forward."

"Wow . . ." Everett rarely found himself at a loss for words, but even he wasn't sure where to go from there. All he'd needed was a bobby pin, but she'd delivered much more. Part of herself. Which was the last thing he wanted. During his early days in the Navy, he'd fallen hard for a woman, only to learn through the grapevine she hadn't wanted a real marriage, but government health and retirement benefits. Since then, he'd adopted a strict no-commitment policy in regard to all members of the fairer sex. How lucky was he that this angel was already committed to the Big Guy? "So then you didn't actually plan on becoming a nun? It just sort of happened?"

She paled as if he'd slapped her, then spun with a flash of red Converse to leave the room. Had he struck a nerve? Maybe that was his *in*?

"Hey!" he shouted after her. "I'm sorry. Come back!"

She did not.

3

Mary Margaret rounded the corner away from her new patient's room and leaned hard against the century-old stone wall, letting the comforting coolness seep through her habit's heavy wool. The last American she'd helped treat was a photographer who, while capturing wildlife stills, had fallen backwards over one of the mountainous region's many cliffs. If local hunters hadn't found him and carried him in, he might have died from a simple break to his right leg. He'd been a nice man. Charles. But nothing about him had turned her insides topsy-turvy and made her forget to breathe.

Why was Everett Black even here? Where had he come from? Why was he cuffed to his bed? Strangers to their area were always a fun topic of mealtime conversation, yet not one of her fellow sisters had spoken a word about this man other than instructing her to regularly take his vitals.

Which reminded her, she'd failed to check his temperature or pulse.

Hugging the man's chart to her chest, she forced her breathing to slow. Clearly, she was still upset by her meeting with Sister Agnes. To so soon after have a stranger casually echo essentially the same sentiments—that the only reason she aspired to be a nun was because she had nowhere else to go and had never known any other life—had been disturbing She loved her life here at the convent and hospital. She loved serving people of all ages. It made her feel as if in some small way, she were a living extension of the precious hand of God.

Eyes closed, she said a quick prayer for forgiveness. She hadn't meant to lose her temper with Everett Black. She returned to his room to take the rest of his vitals. All without saying another word.

That didn't mean she didn't feel the heavy weight of his dark brown stare. Or a strange humming ache throughout her body that came from simply touching her fingers to his wrist to take his pulse. All it really meant was that Mary Margaret was determined to prove herself the best nun anyone had ever seen—starting now, by caring for this man. This awful man who she instinctively knew held the power to unravel parts of her spirit, as if her resolve were no stronger than the yarn from a hand-knitted sweater.

Part of the reason Sister Agnes's kind admonishment had been so upsetting was because deep down, Mary Margaret feared she might be right. And that fact stung.

"I'm sorry." Everett Black's deep voice startled her. "I never meant to dredge up what was obviously a painful part of your past."

She shrugged while adding his pulse to his chart. "It's okay. It happened a long time ago. Now, I try to remember only the good times."

He nodded. "I understand."

As only a select few would, he very well could understand the grief stemming from losing both parents at once. The fact saddened her as much as it joined them in a macabre way.

"Why are you here?" she blurted. "I mean, beyond your injury, why have you come to Piapoco?"

He raised his eyebrows. "You don't know?"

"Why would I?" She nodded to his cuffs. "Are you in some way connected to the drugs that are destroying this country? Are police coming for you?"

"How well do you know the woman who runs this place?"

Her gaze narrowed. "Excuse me?"

"Camilla Rodriguez. Do you know her?"

"Of course, we've met. The señora is one of the kindest, gentlest souls I've ever known. All of this"—she gestured to their surroundings—"wouldn't be possible without her generosity. She's a living saint. Why?"

"Are you sure?"

"Of course. What are you trying to say? Obviously, you're a criminal, so—"

"You're wrong. I'm one of the good guys. Look . . ." As if checking to ensure no one overheard, he peered around her, then lowered his voice to a whisper. "I'm taking a helluva risk in revealing this to you, but your Saint Camilla? She kidnapped my best friend's baby. She was married to one of Colombia's most notorious drug lords."

"You're a liar. Señora Rodriguez is one of the most devout women I've ever known. She would never associate herself with the thugs and killers who make their living from selling death in white powder form. Why are you saying these awful things? What did you do that's so horrible you had to be handcuffed to a hospital bed?"

"I tried to take back my friends' baby. That's it. I'm now being held hostage." She lurched backward when he gave a hard jolt to his restraints. The metallic clang echoed through the rock-walled room.

"*Liar!*" Chin raised, she said, "You are a—"

"*Mary Margaret!*" Sister Agnes stepped up behind

her. "I'm not sure what I just walked in on, and I probably don't care to know. Please go help Sister Catherine prepare the evening meal."

"Yes, Sister." Mary Margaret bowed her head in shame. She had always had a short fuse. It was one of the main sins she whispered to Father Carlos during her confessions. But if there had ever been a reason to be upset with someone, surely, Everett Black's harsh words had been it.

Señora Rodriguez was a saint.

Nothing Everett Black had to say could ever convince Mary Margaret otherwise.

I was told you would be trouble." The older nun looked like the knuckle rapping, pinched-faced parochial school teacher from movies. "From now on, I will personally provide your care."

"Swell . . ." Needing to punch something in frustration, Everett gave an unsatisfying yank to his cuffs. The action only served to make his wrists hurt damn near as bad as his leg. "I need to use the restroom."

Her pale face reddened. Without a word, she took a bulky keychain from the white apron she wore over her black habit. She freed his left hand, then placed a metal bedpan atop his stomach.

He cleared his throat. "I don't mean to be difficult, but I'm right-handed."

"Then I suggest you be careful with your aim." She turned her back on him.

Think, man. With only one hand free, how do I escape this bed?

He eyed the rail that had already proven too solid to break or pull loose. It would be a waste of energy to mess anymore with that. The hairpins holding the current nun's hat in place were also an option, but even if he managed to fling the bedpan at her head hard enough to knock her out, how would he get the pins? And how karmically uncool would it be to knock out a nun?

She asked, "Need assistance?"

"Privacy would be nice."

She headed for the door. "Call when you're done."

Everett searched the room for an advantage he might have missed. Then he saw it—a wall-mounted used needle receptacle. The room was small enough that if he could somehow push himself over the fixed bedrail, then—

"Finished?" The nun cracked open the door.

"Ah, not quite."

She shut the door.

Perfect . . .

Pretending the bed was a gnarly rock face, he used his free arm to push himself up and over the rail. The cuff held his right wrist in a painful contortion he managed to work through. Gritting his teeth, sweat popping on his forehead from pain, he pushed past screaming discomfort to stretch toward the box. His hospital gown gaped open in the back, creating an awkward breeze on his ass and junk. He lunged so far that the antique bed lurched a good six inches, filling the room with the scrape of metal against rock floor.

The door burst open, and the nun peeked through. She took one look at him and screamed, "*Security*! *Help*! Someone call for security!"

Everett froze, but then, in the moment when the nun left him to bolt for the hall, he used the heel of his hand to pop open the plastic box's lid, then reach inside. Pulse racing, he ignored the fact that he was fishing through a vat of used needles to take one before wincing and hobbling his way back to the bed, then vault himself over the rail. Pain radiated past his knee and into his thigh and calf. It actually came as a relief to sink against the cool sheets and pillows.

By the time three, gun-toting security guards exploded into the room, Everett had not only managed to tug the sheet and thin blanket over his bare legs, but take a leak in the bedpan.

"It's about time you guys showed up." He held out the pan. "Mind taking this?"

A conversation erupted between them in

Spanish that was too fast for Everett to make out even a few words.

Four nuns were next to crowd into the cramped space.

More indecipherable conversation erupted. There was much pointing and arguing.

Everett wagged the pan, careful not to slosh. "*Cerveza, por favor?*"

A middle-aged nun he hadn't seen before stepped forward for the pan.

"*Muchas Gracius.*" Everett had no beef with the ladies. They were only doing what they were told. What they thought was right.

More arguing.

Finger pointing.

Two more guards entered. The tallest carried leg restraints.

It was no surprise when Everett found himself surrounded.

While one man tossed back the covers to search the bed, another cuffed Everett's left hand. Two more thugs fastened his legs to the rails.

Everett had expected no less.

Once they'd gotten him good and buckled down, the security team patted themselves on their respective backs for a job well done.

Meanwhile, Everett fingered the needle he'd jammed into the mattress and felt pretty damned good about his own day's work. Now that he had a tool to pick his cuffs, he could essentially leave whenever he wanted. But not without Baby Joe.

An image of the feisty young nun flashed before his mind's eye. What were the odds of converting her to his team?

Low.

But maybe not impossible . . .

Sister Mary Margaret stood at the endless center island in the convent's kitchen, plucking the ends from green beans. The job was tedious, thankless, and hot. The kitchen wasn't air-conditioned like the hospital.

She could count on half of one hand the number of times she'd heard Sister Agnes raise her voice and today had been one of them. Mary Margaret hadn't meant to argue with her patient, but those things he'd been saying about Señora Rodriguez were not only outrageous, but completely unfounded. Somebody had to defend her honor. As for her having kidnapped a baby... The claim was preposterous, and only further proved Mary Margaret's earlier assumption that the man was somehow involved with cocaine. Clearly, he must currently be on it.

"What did you do this time to end up under my

watchful eye?" Sister Catherine was as round as a berry and her flushed cheeks nearly as red. Twice Mary Margaret's age, Catherine was in charge of all meals for the convent and hospital. She oversaw a staff of twelve local men and women, as well as five other nuns. While everything she prepared was delicious, her pastries, cakes, and pies made her as popular as her gentle spirit and easy smile.

Mary Margaret sighed. "It's silly—my own stupid fault. I lost my temper again, only this time, with a patient."

"Uh oh . . ." Sister Catherine rolled out a pie crust on a white marble slab.

"He said horrible things about Señora Rodriguez. I couldn't just stand by and let him sully her good name."

Sister Catherine made no comment. Since she was typically a chatterbox, Mary Margaret found this odd.

"You think I shouldn't have said anything?"

"It's not that . . ." The hesitation in her voice compounded the already awkward situation. "Did you know I voted on the matter of whether or not you were ready to take your formal vows?"

"Yes . . ." Mary Margaret narrowed her gaze. "Sister Agnes told me the decision to deny my request was unanimous."

"It was." Catherine rolled the crust in a perfect layer, then clipped it to fit a clear glass pie plate.

"You know why I think you're not quite ready?"

Mary Margaret shook her head.

"You still see your life through rose-colored glasses. You haven't yet lived long enough to see the world as it truly is. Yes, Señora Rodriguez has done marvelous things for our order and mission, but there are far more layers to her than her charitable work. I fear for you—that once you see that great beauty can often be shadowed by even greater ugliness—you may never fully understand how to discover a balance between the two."

"My parents were murdered. You think I don't know how ugly life can be?"

"Shh . . ." Sister Catherine placed her comforting hand on Mary Margaret's. "Of course, that was an unspeakably tragic time. All I'm saying is for you to arm yourself against naiveté. Even blessings have a price."

Mary Margaret frowned. "Sister, I'm sorry, but I don't understand."

"And I'm not getting these pies baked by standing around chatting."

"But—" Sister Catherine's message made no sense. What was she trying to say?

Why did Everett Black's accusations about Señora Rodriguez have to come on the same day as her latest denial? And now, this cryptic speech? Was God sending her a message? If she were able to make sense of it, might it lead to her finally becoming a full nun?

She'd opened her mouth to ask Sister Catherine this very thing when a commotion near the kitchen's entrance caught her attention.

Camilla Rodriguez, dressed in a white linen pantsuit that made her look cool and lovely despite the heat, chatted with two locally hired women who were chopping green peppers for the evening meal. There was nothing remarkable about that fact. What was remarkable? In her arms, she carried a fussy baby—judging by his blue gingham romper—a boy baby.

A coincidence? Or could this be the infant Everett Black had accused her of taking? Pulse racing uncomfortably fast, Mary Margaret abandoned her green bean snapping station to dash off toward the convent's small orphanage. If the infant was a new arrival, Sister Josephine, who handled the stacks of government paperwork for each child, would know.

And if she didn't?

If Everett Black had told the truth?

Mary Margaret's stomach churned. If the infant had actually been kidnapped, and if he was actually being held against his will and was not a criminal, then she would go straight to Sister Agnes and make sure she contacted the proper authorities to release him.

. . . *Arm yourself against naiveté.*

Sister Catherine's warning rose above the noise of her pounding heart.

In the years Mary Margaret had lived at the convent and worked in the hospital and orphanage, Señora Rodriguez had fully funded both programs— even buying lavish toys, clothes, and entertainment. Tutors in not only primary education, but music and art. The hospital treated villagers from miles away. There was even a new minor surgery wing. How was all of this possible? Where had the money come from to pay for it all?

The more fear and doubt and disillusion swirled in Mary Margaret's confused heart, the more vivid her mind's eye image of Everett Black grew. The urgency with which he'd delivered his message. If she hadn't known better, she might almost have believed his life depended upon her.

But if that were actually true, how far was she prepared to go to help?

4

Jacksonville, Florida

"How is she?"

Nash Adamson looked up from the same magazine article he'd been reading for an hour to find his longtime friends and business associates, Harding and Briggs enter Maisey's cramped Jacksonville Memorial Hospital's ICU room. Up until now, the only noise had been the steady rise and fall of the breathing machine keeping his wife alive. "Still unconscious. Any word from Everett?"

"Negative." Harding stepped closer, planting his hand on Nash's back. "She's gonna pull through. *Believe.*"

Tears stung Nash's eyes. "I'm trying, man. I'm

trying."

Under normal circumstances, Nash was used to being in control. Now? The fate of his wife was in God's hands. As he'd never been one to pray, the thought was unnerving. As for his son?

Briggs had leaned against the far wall. "If Everett hasn't called or popped up on satellite imaging by 0700 tomorrow, Jasper and I are going after him."

Nash nodded. "Thanks."

"No worries. We're in this together and trust me, Vicente's black widow is getting crushed."

Nash closed his eyes, pressing the heels of his hands against them. When the nightmare of saving Maisey and Baby Joe from drug lord Vicente Rodriguez had ended, Nash never saw this scenario coming—of the man's wife not only being hell bent on revenge, but taking back the son she felt was rightfully hers. Only from Nash's point of view, he'd earned the right to help Maisey raise the infant. All Camilla Rodriguez had done was send a couple of hired guns to handle her business. Friends in the DEA said that with so many arrest warrants for her in the States, she'd taken the coward's way out by not daring to show her face.

The custody issue could have been handled a myriad of different ways. Civilized ways.

Maisey had the biggest heart of any woman he'd ever known. Had Camilla asked for supervised visits with her late husband's son, though Nash would have advised against it, Maisey no doubt would have agreed.

Now, however, Nash had lost any interest in playing nice. If the widow wanted a battle, she'd gotten one. If Maisey hadn't been in such serious condition, Nash would have long since gone after their son himself.

"What's the plan?" Nash asked.

Harding said, "Nothing fancy. Your basic aerial insertion, then retracing Everett's trail. With luck, they'll find a local willing to talk. If they hear Everett and your kiddo have been hurt, Jasper and Briggs will have enough firepower to blow Camilla's compound to kingdom come."

Lips pressed tight, Nash nodded.

But honestly? If Maisey woke and discovered so much as one hair on their precious son's head had been harmed, he wouldn't put it past her to hop the next flight to Columbia to take care of business herself.

Mary Margaret left the cheery, yellow-walled orphanage and frowned.

Not even the jubilant shrieks and laughter riding the light breeze from the playground could lighten her suddenly dark mood.

Sister Josephine confirmed her worst fear—that the baby Señora Rodriguez held wasn't an orphan, but her son. She claimed he was her late husband's biological child who had been born from a surrogate mother. According to Josephine, Camilla had never been able to conceive, which was why she and Vicente had turned to surrogacy. Mary Margaret understood that. What confused her was that according to Everett Black, Camilla had kidnapped the infant. But from what Josephine said, the baby was legally hers.

Mary Margaret's head throbbed. None of this made sense.

She had to personally speak to Señora Rodriguez. It was the only move that made sense. The woman had been her savior for over a decade. Mary Margaret at least owed her the courtesy of a conversation before alerting Sister Agnes, and maybe even calling authorities.

Chances were, this was all a misunderstanding.

Mary Margaret dashed from the orphanage to the covered brick walkway leading to the convent's living quarters and kitchen. If she was lucky, Señora Rodriguez would still be there.

Though rushing was discouraged because of its undignified nature, Mary Margaret plowed past gardening and maintenance crews. The late-afternoon air tasted thick on the back of her throat.

Heat and humidity made her wool robe and wimple cling in what Sister Agnes would call an indelicate nature.

"There you are," Sister Catherine said once Mary Margaret huffed and puffed her way back into the kitchen. Two oversized ceiling fans only swirled the hot air. "Where did you run off to in such a hurry?"

"S-Señora Rodriguez? Is she still here?"

"No. She asked me about making special fruit and vegetable purees for her son, then left for the main house."

Only just now catching her breath, Mary Margaret nodded. "Thank you."

Sister Catherine narrowed her gaze. "What are you up to? Why are you flushed? If Sister Agnes caught you in this state, she'd send you straight to bed."

"I'm fine. Really." To prove it, she was already running for the rear exit.

"Mary Margaret!" Sister Catherine bellowed. "Get back here! You never finished the beans!"

Ignoring her superior, Mary Margaret ducked back outside, this time to race toward the castle-like structure she normally only visited for holidays, birthdays, and other special occasions.

Her dash across the impeccably manicured lawn startled three peacocks into a noisy display. She'd almost reached the front entry's heavy wood door when a two-man security team stepped out from behind a corner.

"Sister . . ." A man with pock-marked cheeks and a stinking cigar emerged from the stone entry's deep shadows. "To what do we owe this pleasure?"

"I-I must see Señora Rodriguez. It's a matter of quite some urgency."

"Is she expecting you?"

"No, but—"

Through the entry's towering paned windows came the distinct sound of a baby crying.

"The Señora must not be bothered."

Mary Margaret raised her chin, taking a few steps closer to the door. "My business is urgent. It involves the man being held in the hospital—Everett Black."

"Well, then . . ." The man with the cigar took it from his mouth to squat, grinding the glowing tip against the rock floor. "Wait here. I'll see what I can do."

Lingering sweet smoke turned her stomach.

The man gave Mary Margaret the heebies. He stared right through her.

Once his partner had gone inside, the other guard said, "My sister is a nun. She was shipped off to Bogotá. Can't remember the last time I saw her."

"I'm sorry." Mary Margaret bowed her head. "That must be hard on your family."

The man shrugged.

SHUNNED

The door opened, and the pock-marked guard stood in front of it, gesturing for her to pass through. "Señora is waiting for you in her formal parlor. She said you would know where to go."

"*Si. Gracias.*"

"*De nada.*"

Conditioned air hit Mary Margaret's overheated cheeks like a blessedly cool cloth. The cold felt as unnatural and yet pleasurable as any garden variety sin—maybe more so. She hadn't realized how sticky she'd grown beneath her heavy garments until now, when her fevered flesh cooled.

Led by the sounds of the infant's fitful cries, Mary Margaret's footfalls fell silent on the sumptuous rugs covering the rock floor. Stone walls supported an oil painting gallery lined with sober-faced men and women dressed in historic garb. Heavy wooden armchairs with ruby velvet upholstered seats framed ornately carved side tables topped with brass lamps and dozens of the crystal balls Señora Rodriguez collected. As long as Mary Margaret had lived in the convent, the nuns had joined in to gift the señora with a new piece each birthday and Christmas.

The closer she stepped to the formal room, the more her palms sweated and heart raced. She was doing the right thing in telling Señora what awful claims Everett Black had made, right?

. . . *Arm yourself against naiveté.*

The warning pounded inside her like drums. Was she being naive in believing anything Everett Black had to say? That had to be it. Because she refused to think this woman to whom she owed her very life might be anything other than the living saint she seemed.

Standing in the formal parlor's wide, arched stone entry, Mary Margaret clasped her hands and cleared her throat. "Señora. Thank you for agreeing to see me."

"Of course. I'm always happy to visit with one of my own." She sat on a floral settee that had to be fifteen feet long. Jiggling the baby, cooing into his ear, she looked every bit the part of a mother. "Please, join me. I'm sure my son will soon drift off to dreamland."

"Yes. Of course." Still missing her own mother's hugs, Mary Margaret's eyes stung with unshed tears. Seated, not only did she find the room intimidating with its stone hearth that was big enough to house a small car, but the sweet scent of the coffee table's fresh floral arrangement combined with Señora's rich perfume made her gag . . . No wonder the poor infant was upset. He couldn't breathe.

"My guard says you have something to tell me about our guest?"

"Yes, Señora." *If he's a guest, why is he being restrained to his bed?* "I know of no pleasant way to say this . . ."

"Please . . ." She forced a smile over the infant's louder cries. "Feel free to be frank."

"Everett Black said—" Mary Margaret fisted her skirt's thick wool "—he accused you of kidnapping this infant."

If Mary Margaret hadn't been looking, she might have missed the hitch in Señora's breath or the narrowing of her eyes. She averted her gaze only to spy a small handgun nestled beside the flowers. Why would Señora need a gun?

The señora cleared her throat. "I'm sorry to hear that."

The baby's cries echoed through the vast room. Was he missing his true mother? Could Everett Black's story be true? If so, then the implications ran shockwaves through her entire life. When Sister Catherine had delivered her cryptic speech, could she have been trying to tell Mary Margaret that everything in the convent was not as it seemed?

"In fact, I'm very, very sorry." Señora rose. Cupping the back of the baby's head, she paced in front of the cold stone hearth. "Shh . . ." she whispered to the infant. "No more tears. You are safe. *Home.*"

"Señora?" Mary Margaret also stood, holding out her hands. "Would you like me to take him? I am good with the orphaned infants."

"This is no orphan," the woman practically spat.

"But my son. Go. Never speak of this again or you will meet the same fate as your parents."

What? Confusion clogged Mary Margaret's throat. Why would the señora say such a terrible thing?

"Yes, Señora. As you wish." Mary Margaret bowed her head, backing out of the room.

The infant's cries now sounded more like terror-fueled screams. "Tell Sister Agnes to bring Dr. Garcia right away. My son is sick."

"Yes. Right away." Mary Margaret continued moving backwards until catching her tennis shoe against a rug's edge. She tripped, but caught herself short of falling—not from the rug as she'd assumed, but something far more insidious. A man's feet that had been bound with duct tape stuck out from behind a pair of armchairs.

A glance over her shoulder had her covering her mouth with her hands to keep from retching. His head hung at an unnatural angle—as if his neck had been snapped.

"*Ándale!*" Señora cried. "My son needs the doctor!"

Mary Margaret turned to run.

The baby screamed, fueling her frantic pace.

She should never have come. What had she been thinking? Clearly, she *hadn't* been thinking. Faster and faster she charged down the hall, through the entry and out the front door. She should have called the authorities first. But then if Señora was powerful enough to have kidnapped a child with no one voicing the slightest protest, then who was to say she didn't also control local *policia*?

As for the dead man lying in Señora's formal reception room? Mary Margaret said a quick prayer for God to admit him to Heaven, then forever strike the image from her mind.

Upon her approach, the guards were at first startled to attention, but then laughed—a panicked nun was no threat.

They were wrong.

In the span of a heartbeat, Mary Margaret was naïve no more.

All of the money it took to keep this mecca in the middle of a jungle financially afloat had no doubt been earned by the same drug dealers who had killed her parents. For all she knew, Señora Rodriguez may have been responsible for their deaths. Everett Black had been telling the truth.

That knowledge turned Mary Margaret's veins to ice.

She had to go to him. Everett. She had to enlist his help in returning this poor, frightened baby safely back into his true mother's arms.

Would she ever find her own place in this foreign, upside down world? She was terrified she might never know.

5

"Swear on your eternal soul that what you told me about Señora Rodriguez's baby being kidnapped is true."

Having been knocked out by the contents of a mystery syringe, Everett couldn't be sure if the pretty young nun actually stood at the foot of his bed, backlit by a yellow halo of light, or if she were merely a dream.

"Answer me. If it is true, we don't have much time."

Everett wanted to answer, but his tongue felt thick.

"Are you okay? What's wrong?" She stepped closer. Close enough that with his newly freed hands, if he'd had the energy, Everett could have bolted upright to grab her—to see for himself if she felt as soft and kissable as she looked—not that he would kiss her. Just sayin'. He'd picked his cuff locks just prior to the needle-happy nun's visit, then he'd clasped them loosely enough around his wrists to slip free when the time was right. "Were you sedated?"

He nodded. At least he thought he had been?

She sighed, then tilted her face upward. "God, in the years I've spent devoted to You, I haven't asked for much, but could You please make something during the course of this endless day go right?"

Taa daa! Everett yanked his hands free, wagging his fingers in what he hoped was an appropriately messiah-like way.

"I swear . . ." She made the sign of the cross on her chest. Under her breath, she muttered while unlatching the man's leg restraints, "You will either be my savior or damnation. I had hoped you'd help with the baby, but in your current condition, you're not much more aid to me than a small child."

She maneuvered a wheelchair alongside the bed, then removed a bundle of clothes from the seat. "I brought jeans and a T-shirt, along with socks and shoes. I could only guess at the size. I can't even imagine how much trouble I'll be in for stealing them from the laundry."

You're beautiful, he wanted to say to his angel. *Thank you.*

Approaching the head of the bed, she tugged

down his covers, then reached out to touch his shoulders, as if she planned on removing his hospital gown, but had second thoughts. As a nun, she couldn't have seen many male chests. Not to be cocky, but his was a damned fine specimen.

Still not entirely sure this wasn't all a dream, Everett found the energy to raise his arms, giving the gown a yank. It wasn't tied around his neck, and when cool air kissed his pecs, the poor girl's cheeks turned hibiscus red.

Averting her gaze, she held out a green T-shirt. "Think you can manage to slip this on?"

"Yeah," he said with a painful grunt when his arms ached from having been forced into the same position for too long. He rode out the cramps, then got his head stuck in an arm hole. "Help?"

She leaped to his side, inadvertently skimming her warm, nimble fingers across his neck and biceps and abs. As much as he'd enjoyed her touch, she seemed traumatized by their brief contact. Usually women loved touching him. This pretty nun was hell on his ego. "I, um, didn't think to bring undergarments."

"I—" His mouth was painfully dry. His tongue still protested having to work. As if reading his mind, she poured water from a nearby pitcher into a plastic cup, then held it to his parched lips. After drinking his fill, he winced, then said, "Thanks."

"You're welcome. But we must hurry."

"What time is it?"

"Late enough for most everyone to be sleeping, but that doesn't mean danger isn't everywhere."

"W-why are you helping me?"

"I'll explain later. For now, let's get you dressed and to the van. Once I get the baby, we will leave and drive to Medellin. From there, we'll plan our next move." She tossed jeans onto the bed, gesturing for him to put them on.

He nodded. She was a smart cookie.

Just one more thing he found attractive about her.

The faded jeans she slipped past his feet and ankles were soft from no doubt many washings. She wrestled them up to his knees, then turned away. "I trust you can manage from here?"

"Sure." It was hell working them over his bum knee, but if she hadn't been able to deal with the sight of his bare chest, she sure wasn't ready for his package. Still partially covered by the sheet and blanket, he lifted his ass to pull the jeans all the way up. After fastening the waistband button and pulling up the zipper, he said, "Done."

As if he were a child, she slipped thick white socks onto his feet for him, and then tan leather work boots. "Do you think your leg has healed well enough for you to drive?"

"Sure—as long as it's not a stick."

She winced. "I'm afraid that's all we have. It's the van we use for outings."

"It'll be fine," he assured her. *Sort of.* He was

great at most things, but driving a standard transmission? Not so much. Toss in the added fun of his left knee being on fire, and it was a guaranteed shit show. Still, riding out a little pain was the least he could do in return for this woman's rescue. "If you don't mind my asking, how are you planning on getting the baby?"

She was back at it with crossing her chest. "Luck. Lots and lots of luck."

Mary Margaret was amazed by how smoothly she'd been able to wheel Everett Black out of the hospital's back entry, down the covered walkway leading to the convent's small parking area, and then help settle him behind the van's wheel.

She'd expected security to show up around every corner, but so far, they'd encountered no one. It was two in the morning, so she shouldn't have been surprised, but as loud as her heart was beating, she'd assumed everyone within a five-mile radius would hear.

"Wait," she said after handing him the keys she'd stolen from the cookie jar where Sister Catherine kept important things.

"Look . . ." Before she shut the door, he grabbed her forearm. Her sleeve had risen and the feel of his fingers against her bare skin wreaked havoc on her already panicked system. She knew she should pull away, but oddly lacked the wherewithal to perform the action. "Now that I'm coming out of my drug fog, let me help. We'll get the baby together."

The thick night air smelled of approaching rain. A lightning flash, followed by rolling thunder promised a coming storm.

"Impossible." She shook her head, then finally managed to free herself from his pleasurable hold. "Security in Señora's home is tight. When guards stop my entry, I will say I'm bringing medicine for the baby to sleep. Once inside, I will either be able to take the infant or not. Obviously, until reaching his room, I have no way of knowing how many guards protect him. Please watch for me. If I succeed, I will be running toward you from that direction." She pointed over her left shoulder. "On the other hand, should you hear a commotion or God forbid—gunfire—then you will know I failed. At that point, save yourself."

He arched his head back and groaned. "I don't like this. I should be saving the baby and you."

"I appreciate the offer, but in case you failed to notice, I just rescued you."

Lightning cracked. Thunder shook the ground.

"See?" she found the courage to tease. "Even my boss agrees."

"Do me a favor?"

"What?"

"I know we hardly know each other, but be careful."

"You, too. And remember what I said—if you sense something went wrong, please go. Bring back help for your friends' son."

"Sister?" He was again reaching for her, but she backed away. "Geez, I don't even know your name."

"Mary Margaret. We will have plenty of time to get acquainted during the next leg of our journey."

Before she chickened out by taking him up on his offer to help, Mary Margaret crept into the shadow provided by the orphanage's bus. She'd tried her best to come across strong, but inside, she was a mess. Could she really do this? Take Señora Rodriguez's baby boy?

Her dear parents' smiling faces flashed before her mind's eye.

Then, the empty gaze of the dead man she'd stumbled over.

Steeling her shoulders, more determined than ever to see this through, Mary Margaret reasoned that logically, this was a task she was uniquely suited to do. Even if both of Everett Black's legs were in perfect working order, she sensed that he lacked the finesse to ever pass Señora's personal army.

She clung to the garage's shadows until reaching the convent's main housing unit.

From there, she quietly entered, forced a deep, calming series of breaths, then plunged forward down the dark halls leading past the kitchen, offices, and chapel where they performed morning prayers. Mary Margaret craved to stop in for a quick pep talk from the Lord, but there was no time. The baby must be returned to his mother. The poor soul had to be out of his mind with fear.

Outside, lightning and growling thunder alerted her that the storm grew closer. Inside, a cyclone of broken emotions frightened her far more than mere rain and wind. *If* she accomplished returning this infant to his rightful mother, Mary Margaret would then have nowhere else to go. Our Mother of the Blessed Angel was the only home she'd ever known. She would be shunned by her friends and church. Was righting Señora Rodriguez's heinous wrong worth the havoc this act would wreak upon her carefully ordered life?

Yes.

Wind-driven rain pelted the windows, propelling her into action.

Just outside the downstairs bathroom was a supply closet where basic medical items were stored. Aspirin and bandages. Antiseptic and soothing sunburn spray. She flipped on the overhead light to find a bottle of ear drops. They were meant for Sister Helen's occasional bouts of swimmer's ear, but the guard didn't have to know that. She tore off the brown glass bottle's exterior label, tucked the paper in her right skirt pocket, then the bottle in her left.

Operating on pure adrenaline, she exited the

closet to find herself still alone.

Upon soundlessly closing the closet door, she tiptoed further down the hall, trying not to be creeped out by the play of lightning-strobed shadows springing to macabre life on every wall.

She'd almost reached the convent's rear exit when a voice called from the darkness. "Mary Margaret? Why are you up so late?"

"I, ah . . ." While dreaming up an answer for Sister Agnes, Mary Margaret's heart thundered louder than the storm. In her pocket, her sweating palm brushed the cool bottle. "Have an earache." She waved the medicinal proof. "There's hardly any left, so I thought I'd take it to my cell." Ironic—the name of the small spaces where the nuns slept. For most of her life, Mary Margaret had considered her own closet-like space a sanctuary, but now, realizing how she'd been living under layer upon layer of lies, she truly had been trapped in a cell of her own making.

"I'll say a prayer for you, my child." She gestured for Mary Margaret to join her on the walk up the rear staircase to their cells. "Come. A good night's rest is oftentimes the best medicine."

"True." Mary Margaret forced a smile. *Do I look as guilty as I feel?* "Thank you for your prayer. I'll, ah, be up as soon as I get a glass of water."

"Of course." Sister Agnes bowed her head, then thankfully exited up the stairs.

Just in case she returned, Mary Margaret did go

to the kitchen, but rather than drinking water, she indulged in several long pulls from the corked, sweet red wine usually reserved for feasting days.

Wind and driving rain rattled the windows.

Thunder shook the stone walls, making them feel no longer solid, but as precarious as her future.

The room's only light was the dim fixture above the sink. It flickered, then went out.

In this remote region, power outages were common. The generators would soon kick on.

Mary Margaret held her breath—waiting for the familiar chug of powerful diesel engines banishing the dark of night. But when there was no sound other than thunder and wind-driven rain, her panic rose to new heights. Maybe the storm was a good thing? Maybe the chaos would provide just the cover she needed to take the infant without being discovered?

Deciding God might be on her side, she gulped the kitchen's hot, sticky air, then took off running. Ignoring the rain, the way the moisture soaked her wool habit, weighting her every step, she ran until her lungs felt near bursting, then pushed still harder.

She approached Señora's mansion by the rear service entry. Many times she had used the security code needed to open the door. She punched in the familiar numbers, but the green light remained unlit. In fact, the entire panel was dark.

She tugged the usually locked door. It swung open.

She released the breath she'd been holding, then crept into the dark service area. Washable rubber mats protected the stone and her footfalls. She assumed the infant would be in the north wing, near Señora's personal suite.

Mary Margaret's worst fear was that the baby would stay in the same room as his temporary mother. If this fear proved true, she was unsure of what to do. For now, her only hope was to remain undetected for as long as possible by the guards whose low voices she heard in another room.

They argued about who was in charge of the generator.

As far as Mary Margaret was concerned, it could stay off.

She'd been to the mansion enough that lightning flashes guided her up the back stairs to the second floor. On the landing, her pounding heart told her to beware of guards, but curiously, there were none.

This is too easy, her ragged breaths said with each step.

The mansion's second floor hall seemed endless. The décor was much the same as the lower hall, only creepy family portraits had been replaced by equally gloomy oil landscapes—some in ornate, gilded frames as large as refrigerators.

Her wet skirts dragged atop the priceless antique rugs. Her sodden wimple and veil made her feel off balance and awkward. She would have loved to rip it off, but couldn't. It was inevitable that she would encounter guards, which meant maintaining her usual outer appearance.

She began searching room after room, but there was no sign of the baby.

The closer she came to the double doors leading to Señora's suite, the more Mary Margaret fought panic. What was she doing? How would she ever pull this off?

With still no guard present, she held her breath while turning one of the crystal knobs.

The door soundlessly swung open.

Lightning illuminated a terrifying scene. Not only was the infant in the room, but held in Señora's arms. While he softly whimpered, Señora sang a Spanish lullaby.

A trio of antique silver candelabras had been lit. They each held twelve white candles that lent the room an eerie, flickering glow.

Aborting the mission, Mary Margaret took a backward step. It proved a catastrophic mistake. She'd forgotten that the mansion's upper floors were wood. When she'd stepped, the floor creaked, giving away her presence.

"Who's there?" Señora swung to face her. Gaze narrowed, she asked, "Mary Margaret. Why are you out in this storm?"

6

Jacksonville, Florida

"Nurse! Help! My wife, she . . ." Nash's words trailed off while a team of nurses ran from their station to Maisey's intensive care room.

He'd been on his laptop, trying to catch up on business by her bedside, when all hell had broken loose. Buzzing and beeps erupted from her many monitors and she'd arched her back, clawing at her face, desperate for her next breath.

For as long as he lived, he'd never forget her terror-filled expression.

Even worse, his own feelings of helplessness. Regret.

If only he'd entered their dark home before her.

If only he'd been fast enough to catch the men who'd taken their son. If only he'd had the foresight to have had Vicente Rodriguez's widow checked out before any of this had even gone down.

Leaning against the wall outside of Maisey's room, Nash pressed the heels of his hands hard against his forehead.

If Maisey died . . .

If Camilla Rodriguez harmed their son . . .

If Everett had fallen victim to her goon squad . . .

What? What the hell was he going to do from here? He balled his hands into fists. Never had Nash felt more helpless. More at the mercy of his friends to right impossible wrongs.

At first, one nurse left Maisey's room, then another and another, all giving him pitying glances.

One blond RN who Harding was always chatting up patted Nash's shoulder. What was her name? Olivia? "Deep breaths. Your wife is a fighter. Turns out she just had a kink in one of her hoses. If I have anything to say about it, she's going to be fine."

"Thanks."

"My pleasure."

"Can I go back in?"

"Of course." She turned toward the nurses' station. "Let me grab a refill for her IV solution, and I'll be back in to bug both of you."

"Sounds good." Nash's chest hadn't felt this

tight with terror since—well, it was around about the same time he and Maisey had rediscovered each other. They'd had Rodriquez's men chasing them down and had been surrounded by snakes and gators and muggy air filled with more mosquitoes than oxygen. If they'd somehow managed to make it through all of that, then they'd damn well survive this latest assault.

But what happens if Maisey doesn't pull through? What happens if your baby never comes home?

Tears stinging his eyes, Nash clutched Maisey's hand. "Live. *Please*, my love, just live.

7

Piapoco, Colombia

"Aw, hell . . ." Everett had known this escape plan was going too good to last.

Through the van's rain-soaked windshield, he spied a cluster of guards.

Lightning revealed seven of them—each carrying enough firepower to take out a small village.

Though the drum of rain on the van's roof prevented him from hearing what they were saying, their animated gestures didn't take much translation. Either they'd discovered he was missing or that the nun had taken the baby. Maybe both.

Regardless, time to enact Plan B.

Everett wasn't yet sure what that was, but it sure

as hell didn't entail sitting here like some stooge, waiting to be made. His own personal angel had gone to a lot of trouble to save him, and he'd do his damnedest to save her right back.

He took the keys from the ignition, pocketed them, then inched open the door, wincing when it creaked. Even under the storm's ferocious cover, every sound could expose him. For whatever nefarious reason, Camilla Rodriguez had kept him alive this long, but in the future, she might not be so generous.

The foot attached to his bum knee was first to hit the ground. He bit his tongue hard enough to draw blood, but fought through the pain. He'd been in worse jams. This was nothing.

He hobbled from the van to an open-sided shed that not only provided shelter from the rain pelting his face, but offered a variety of gardening tools he could use for both a cane and weapon. The stale air inside smelled of grass clippings and mower fuel.

Opting for a pitchfork, he gripped the smooth wooden handle, using its strength to get him from one side of the long, shallow structure to the other.

This new vantage afforded him a full-range view of the backs of the convent and mansion. When his angel emerged with Baby Joe, he'd provide cover.

And if she didn't—emerge?

He grimaced through a nauseating wave of pain. Failure had never been an option before, and he sure as hell didn't plan on making it one now.

Cloaked in protective shadows, he watched the guards divide into teams of two, then spread out, presumably to search the estate for him.

The one lone guard strode toward the van to which Everett held the keys. If the guy had been well-trained, by shining his halogen flashlight through the windows, he'd find the seat partially wet—a telltale sign someone had recently opened the door. From there, Everett's boots had left deep imprints in the rich tropical soil. Yes, the rain would steadily wash prints away, but not fast enough. Plus, the lightning and thunder had lessened, meaning, as with most tropical storms, the downpour would be short-lived.

Pulse steady, leaning against the shed's weathered wood wall, Everett regulated his breathing while waiting to see if the guard was any good. Unfortunately, he was. All too soon, the lanky figure used his flashlight to trace Everett's path.

Everett leaned deeper into the shadows, waiting for the guard's approach.

His boots crunched across the shed's dry gravel floor.

The original plan had been to stab him with the pitchfork, but on second thought, not only would it be messy and take a lot of effort to ram the spikes through the guard's protective armor, if Everett missed, that gave the guy ample opportunity to call *friends.*

With the rain now a sprinkle, any sound would carry. Everett couldn't take the chance.

Searching his surroundings, he found shelves filled with clay pots and fertilizer. Spades and insecticides. The one useable item was a box of trash bags. He grabbed it, found it nearly full, and smiled.

After silently withdrawing a black plastic bag, he opened it, then waited . . .

And waited . . .

And when the poor bastard stepped within reach, Everett used the element of surprise to his advantage. Lunging from the shadows, he ballooned the bag over the man's head, drew it tight around his neck, then held it in place until the man lost the will and air to struggle.

With the guard's body still twitching, Everett dropped him, stripped him of his weapons, then squinted into the inky night.

The storm had passed, leaving the air eerily still. The guards' animated voices carried from all corners of the estate.

Angel, where are you? What's taking so long?

Everett was debating whether or not to launch a search for her when shots rang out.

A woman screamed. His angel?

His nice, chill heart rate? Gone.

The storm returned full force, only this time, hammering in his chest. He barely knew the woman, but if something had happened to her . . .

"Mary Margaret," the señora repeated. "Why are you out in this storm?"

"I, um," her tongue refused to work. *Think. Say anything.* "When the generators failed to come on, I was worried about you and your sweet baby. Is everything all right?"

"Yes. Of course. Although it was kind of you to think of me. Look at you. Even in this dim light, I can see you are soaked." Having never seen the proud woman without her makeup and tailored clothes, it came as a shock to Mary Margaret to find her looking not only older than usual, but defeated. "Let me put down the baby and get you a towel."

"T-that's not necessary," Mary Margaret said. "I don't mean to be a bother."

"Hush. It's no trouble at all. Actually, you'd be doing me a favor. As you can hear, my *cariño* still isn't feeling his best. I've been walking with him for hours and would love a hot soak. Would you mind watching him? Promise, I won't be long."

Feeling as if angels had orchestrated the entire event, Mary Margaret nodded. "Of course. Please. Take all the time you need."

"Bless you. But first, I'll get your towel." She

placed the baby in a canopy-covered crib, then took one of the candelabras with her to what Mary Margaret knew from past glimpses to be a marble palace of a bathroom.

A knock sounded on the outer door.

"Señora?" called a muffled male voice.

"Mary Margaret, would you be so kind as to see what Fernando wants?"

"Of course." She made the sign of the cross. Just when her mission to take the baby had seemed doable, with the appearance of the chief of Señora's security detail, now her task once again seemed impossible. Her wet habit made each step torture. The wool rubbed her skin raw.

Or maybe that was her guilty conscience?

She was on the verge of breaking a woman's heart. Even though this act was justified, it didn't come without an emotional price.

Mary Margaret had known the señora since she'd been a child. She hated this terrible informational burden Everett Black had placed upon her. Even worse, she hated the shame of only just now realizing the señora was no saint, but a monster. Sister Agnes was right to have denied Mary Margaret's final vows. She was not worthy. But then how were any of them? The entire convent had operated for decades under what were essentially layers of lies upon lies.

Terror froze her limbs. Pinned her feet to the

floor.

"Señora, please." Fernando knocked again. "I must speak with you."

Mary Margaret pressed her hands over her runaway heart, then glanced over her shoulder to ensure the señora had already entered the bathroom. She had. The sound of running water carried past the closed door.

Shoulders straight, more determined than ever to see this mission successfully through, Mary Margaret adopted Mother Superior's haughty pose, then marched to face the head of Señora's security. "It is late," she said upon jerking open the door. "The señora is exhausted from caring for her baby. Mother and child finally find a moment of peace and you have the audacity to disturb them?"

"Sister." The man bowed his head. "I did not know you were here."

"Of course, I am here. Señora needed my help. Now, tell me your business and as soon as she is well enough to hear, I shall relay your news."

He peered past her. Presumably to check if all was right within the lavish suite? He carried a large gun, and had another holstered on his hip. The image of that afternoon's dead man flashed in her mind's eye.

"Well?" Mary Margaret feared her knees buckling from terror, yet rage notched her chin higher. Could this be the very man who had pulled the trigger on her parents?

"Tell Señora our . . . *guest*, has escaped. We are searching for him now, and feel confident he can't have gone far."

"Very well. I will deliver your message. Although I am certain she will not be pleased."

The man's gaze narrowed. "Are you sure the señora's okay? Should I sweep her room?"

"While she's indisposed?" Mary Margaret feigned shock. "I should think not. Now, go, before you wake her baby."

"Yes." As if confused by Mary Margaret's transformation from scared mouse to confident eagle, the man stroked his thick black mustache. He unclipped a small, handheld radio from his belt, and handed it to her. "If you or the señora see our guest, please let me know. I am afraid he will once again try taking her son."

"Of course." She bowed her head. "I will guard the infant with my very life."

"Thank you, Sister." The exchange ended as abruptly as it had begun. Fernando retreated into the mansion's gloom, and once his heavy footfalls echoed down the marble stairs, she dared breathe.

Before she had time to think of any one of the hundreds of ways taking the señora's baby could go wrong, she forced herself to envision the infant's reunion with his true mother.

She cautiously approached the crib, her hands

hovering just shy of the infant's tiny form when the bathroom door lurched open.

Mary Margaret jolted back.

"Is he okay?" Señora asked.

"Of course. You startled me." *Was this it? The moment when she was caught and killed like that mystery man downstairs? Like her parents?* Her heart beat to an alarming degree.

Señora handed Mary Margaret a thick white towel, then leaned over the side of the crib, running her hand along the fitfully sleeping infant's backside. "Thank you again for your help. I won't be long."

As quietly as she'd appeared, the señora left.

Knowing she must take the baby now or never, Mary Margaret tossed the towel over her habit's still soaked shoulder, then scooped the infant from his crib. "You'll be home soon," she promised.

Spying a diaper bag on the floor near a changing table, she crammed it full of as many supplies as it would hold, then ran.

The sudden action resulted in a burst of tears— not just from the infant, but Mary Margaret. Knowing if she was to have a chance at a clean escape, neither the señora or guards must hear. She ducked into one of a half-dozen guest rooms, took a throw blanket from the foot of a bed, then tossed it over her wailing charge.

With his cries at least muffled, she dashed down the darkened hall, praying the lights stayed off long enough for her to reach the van where Everett waited.

She reached the back staircase, painstakingly finding her way in the suffocating black. At any moment, Fernando or one of his thugs could find her, dragging her back to the señora for the sort of punishment she was too scared to even imagine.

Every step felt like descending a mountain. Each exhalation, as if she were releasing a part of herself. This place, these people, were part of her, yet none of them were as they'd seemed. When she'd had nowhere else to go, she'd believed and trusted each and every one of them, but it had all been a lie. And for what? Glorification and money?

The thought not only raised bile in the back of her throat, but hastened her footsteps until she finally reached the bottom landing.

The storm had passed and faint moonlight shone like a beacon to the kitchen's service entry.

Adrenaline propelled her forward until she was pushing open the door, diving for freedom.

I did it! Elation and relief and a myriad of other emotions she didn't fully comprehend swept through her as she jogged down the stone path leading around the back of the mansion to the convent.

She had almost reached the fork where the path veered toward the service buildings and garage when a dark figure stepped off the convent's side porch.

SHUNNED

The glowing red tip of his cigar and its sticky-sweet smell alerted Mary Margaret to the fact that this was the same guard who had initially blocked her from seeing the señora.

"Sister." He bowed his head. "Where are you off to in such a hurry? Especially with the señora's child, at this time of night?"

8

Moonlight showed the terror on his angel's features.

Baby Joe's cries were loud enough to wake the dead and any other guards in the vicinity. Not thinking, just doing, from beneath the bush where he'd taken cover, Everett took out the guard with one shot between his beady black eyes.

It was thoughtful of their hostess to have equipped her security team with an assortment of weapons—even a DTA SRS outfitted with a TBAC noise suppressor.

His angel shrieked, then took off running toward the van where Everett was supposed to have been waiting.

"Hold up!" he called, scrambling out from

under the bush as fast as his injury allowed. "It's me."

"I-I told you to stay in the van." Despite the sticky heat, her teeth chattered. *Shock?*

"Yeah, well, I suspect like you, following directions has never been my strong suit. Come on . . ." Gritting his teeth against what felt like shards of glass cutting at the tendons around his knee, Everett took the heavy baby bag from his angel, then led her to their ride.

At the van, he said, "Since we don't have an infant seat, how about you sit in back."

Her eyes loomed huge and glassy. Everett had seen this look before on innocent locals in the Middle East who'd had the misfortune of being caught between the good guys and the government du jour. The look typically signaled the man, woman, or child having checked out. But in this case, Everett needed his angel with him.

He popped open the passenger-side rear door, gesturing for her to climb in.

When she didn't, he tossed the bag on the floorboard, then, bracing himself as best he could against the van's side, hefted her and the baby onto the seat before buckling her in.

She was soaked. Shivering. Her teeth chattered.

Obviously, his first order of business was to get them far from the compound. But after that, he had to get her dry. Who knew how long of a journey they had ahead of them to smuggle the baby out of a country that Camilla Rodriguez practically owned. For however long it took, he needed his angel in good shape.

"Look," he said, after fastening her seat belt, "I know this has to have been rough for a woman of your stature, but you did good. Real good. I'm going to get us out of here—hopefully, without drawing more attention, then—"

Too late.

A trio of guards rounded the convent's south corner, spotted Everett, then charged—guns blazing.

"Get down!" The time for being gentle had passed. He shoved her as low as the seat belt allowed.

Baby Joe wailed.

It took superhuman strength for Everett to close the nun's door, then somehow get himself behind the wheel.

He reached into his jeans front pocket for the keys, only they weren't there.

Shit.

Had they fallen out when he'd been under the bush?

From outside came the muffled sounds of shouting in heated Spanish.

Everett ignored it all long enough to hotwire the thankfully ancient van. The engine chugged to life.

SHUNNED

Why the goon squad hadn't just shot out the tires Everett didn't know, but he wasn't complaining. Punching the clutch was a real treat to his screwy knee, but even with sweat popping out on his brow, he managed.

Bullets struck the windshield, shattering the tempered glass.

While Baby Joe wailed and the angel shrieked, Everett leaned forward, using the heel of his hand to knock out enough glass for him to at least see where the hell he was going.

He made it out the estate's massive iron electronic gates just before they closed, then intuitively turned north, toward the Jeep he'd stashed during what now felt like another lifetime. How had it only been a couple days?

Knowing he had like three minutes tops before Camilla's gang mobilized and gave chase, Everett needed a radical escape plan—*fast*.

The region was mountainous to the extreme with thick forest lining both sides of a narrow dirt— mostly mud—road. Under ordinary circumstances, he'd have had time to study every detail from which locals could be trusted down to which plants could be eaten in a pinch.

Now, he had nothing to rely on but luck and his own ingenuity.

His Jeep and supply stash were still a good four miles away. He floored the van's accelerator, but slowed when the vehicle fishtailed on the road's slimy surface.

Low-hanging clouds had rolled in, not only blocking moonlight, but the landmark he'd established for finding his ride. A huge rock outcropping that had reminded him of an old Chevy he'd once owned. Not far from there, the road launched into a series of hairpin curves with sheer drop-offs. If he could find the damned Jeep, he just might have a way to get Camilla's goons off their trail long enough to get to a phone so he could arrange for an extraction. His sat phone had been taken along with all of his other primary supplies by Camilla's welcoming committee.

"You know they will find us." From the backseat, his angel's voice barely carried above the van's chugging engine and baby's fitful cries.

"Maybe." He shrugged. "I'm not gonna lie, the odds aren't exactly in our favor, but what you did in getting the baby safely from the compound was huge. With that accomplished, all we have to do now is get him home to Florida."

"Piece of cake, right?" Her laughter bordered on hysteria. "It just occurred to me that I don't even have a passport. And how do we sneak an infant out of a country when he has no papers or parents?"

"Let me handle that. I have friends in seriously great places. All I need you to do is grab the baby and his gear, then jump when I say."

"E-excuse me? Jump where?"

He glanced in the rearview, Instead of the rapidly approaching headlights he'd anticipated, he saw nothing but darkness. *Sweet*.

"Mr. Black? Where, exactly, am I supposed to jump?"

"Call me Everett. And trust me, as soon as I can see far enough through this pea soup to find where I hid my ride, you'll be the first to know." He squinted into the ghostly white.

"If you'd tell me what exactly you're looking for, I could help."

"A rock that looks like a Chevy."

She sighed. "We're all going to die."

"Oh, ye of little faith. What kind of nun are you?"

"H-honestly? I'm not really a nun at all . . ." Her words trailed into an ugly, crying-sob combo that tore at his guts. "Mother Superior and the high council never voted me s-suitable for taking my final vows."

Damn. He wasn't sure what that meant, but anyone who didn't think this sweetheart was good enough to make a great nun could suck it. "Sorry."

"It's okay. I mean, it's not, but—" He glanced over his shoulder to find her covering her face with her hands. "After this whole mess, it's not like I could go back to the church even if I wanted to."

"Not to change the subject, because I really am

sorry that by helping me you've screwed your entire future, but remember how I told you to be ready to jump?"

"Now?"

"Yeah." He stopped the van. The rock form he'd been looking for loomed from the mist. "Just climb the hill and the Jeep is parked in a mass of wax palms. If I don't come back, keys are under the driver's seat. There's a tarp over it, but if you're looking, you can't miss it."

"What's a wax palm? And w-where are you going?" She clutched Baby Joe to her chest, then hoisted the diaper bag over her shoulder.

"Don't worry about it. Just stay—" *Shit.* Headlights backlit the fog. Arguing voices carried. "Go! I'll catch up."

"But—"

"*Go!*" Before she was even all the way out, he tried gunning the engine, but excruciating knee pain made him pop the damn clutch.

Ruh, ruh, ruh.

Ruh, ruh, ruh.

When the van's engine refused to start, Everett released a string of curses, but then stopped. He needed help from the big man Himself. No need in further pissing Him off.

Slamming the heel of his hand against the wheel, he tried one more time. When the engine chugged to life, he winced through the process of slipping it into gear, then lurching down the road, praying his angel and the baby were safe.

He released a long, slow exhale.

Back in business. But for how long?

The lights in the rearview were no longer diffused by the fog, but distinct. He'd have one chance to make this work. If it didn't? Well, he'd just have to revert back to *having* to make it work. Failure wasn't an option.

He gunned the van as fast as he dared on the unforgiving road surface. Then, at the next hairpin turn, he sucked in as much air as his lungs would hold before taking a literal leap of faith . . .

9

The explosion shook the earth hard enough to make Mary Margaret slip and lose her footing.

Mr. Black!

Panic surged through her in drowning waves. This couldn't be happening. He had to be okay. But logic told her he wasn't. No one could survive such a violent explosion.

An agonized sob escaped her. *Why?* Mr. Black was such a good soul. How could he have been taken from her before they'd ever even . . . What? Held hands? Kissed? Gotten to know each other the way a man and woman should?

She was acting crazy. She'd hardly known him. Yet with every breath in her body, she felt as if she'd always known him and he'd now been stolen.

SHUNNED

The baby cried louder than ever, so she paused behind the rock's shelter. Dropping the diaper bag, she swaddled him in the relatively dry towel, then gathered her composure long enough to rock him into a fitful sleep.

How could he be gone? How could he be gone? The phrase played on endless repeat through her head and heart.

Silent tears streamed down her cheeks as she pondered the unfathomable selfless action Everett Black had just performed.

He had died so that she might live, thereby returning this innocent babe to his mother and father. Her throat and heart ached for the man she'd hardly known, yet on some unfathomable, soul-deep level, mourned.

Never had she felt more alone.

Despair settled into her heart like a cold rain.

The van's plummet over the edge of the sheer cliff had resulted in a fire ball hot enough to burn off a section of fog. At the cliff's edge stood the señora's entire security brigade, arms folded in front of four Hummers. They'd left the headlights on, and it looked as if several were hooking themselves in to rappelling gear.

"*Son todos muertos!*" One of the men called into the night.

Muertos. Dead. Just as Everett had planned, they believed all three of them had died—not just him.

Mary Margaret prayed for his dear soul.

Prepared to complete his goal of returning the infant to his parents, Mary Margaret turned from the grisly scene to shift away a portion of the Jeep's cover. She would not dare leave until all of Señora's security team had gone. But until then, she climbed inside the vehicle for shelter from the rapidly cooling temps. To cry out her grief without fear of attracting unwanted attention.

She owed Everett Black a very steep debt. If it was the last thing she ever did, she planned to pay that debt in full.

Everett's entire body trembled from the effort of hanging onto the sheer rock face with his fingertips. He loved climbing. His entire adult life, he'd climbed for work and pleasure. But swear to God, if he survived this night, if he never saw another rock, it would be too soon.

When he'd jumped from behind the van's wheel, he'd underestimated its speed, meaning that instead of landing with a painful thump in the road's mud, he'd arced over the cliff alongside his ride. If his shirt hadn't caught on a scraggly tree growing out of the side of the mountain, he'd have been splattered.

He might still be if he lost his grip before outlasting his welcoming committee. They stood at the cliff's edge about fifty feet above, engaged in a heated debate over what his pathetic Spanish told him involved how they would tell their boss that her son and the gringos who took him were apparently dead.

A low rumble of thunder signaled the approach of another storm.

Lightning showed Everett poised about fifteen horizontal feet from a narrow ledge.

Gritting his teeth, muscles screaming, he inched in that direction until his fingertips stung from dime-sized blisters that popped into a matching set of ten bleeding wounds. Good times. He told himself he'd been through worse, but at the moment, he was hard pressed to remember when.

As if God had turned on a faucet, rain fell in wind-driven sheets. Pelting his face, and making the already impossible task that much harder when the rocks grew even more slippery beneath his touch.

Lightning struck too close for comfort.

The resulting boom made him jerk, and come too damned close to losing his already failing grip.

He made the mistake of looking down. If he so much as sneezed, it'd be lights out. Shit, shit, *shit*.

Teeth chattering from cold, fingers and arms dangerously close to numb, he finally reached the ledge, then dragged himself on top of it, not even caring that as he lay prone, trying to catch his breath, the rocky cradle was filling with enough water that if he passed out, he'd be in the new but very real danger of drowning.

Hypothermia was another likely way he could go.

And that was assuming the guys above him didn't wise up to the fact that they'd been duped by his classic diversionary plan.

Once Everett's breathing evened, he pushed himself onto his knees, then scrambled beneath a slim overhang. It provided zero protection from the cold, but some from the driving rain.

He closed his eyes and saw her. His angel.

Was she okay? Had she found the Jeep?

How was Baby Joe?

Exhaustion settled in. His thoughts drifted to the kinds of things best left alone. Like the realization that if his angel was no longer a nun, he might—just might—stand a narrow chance of getting to know her in the way a man and woman should. In the process, he might be forced to break his no-commitment rule, but at least it'd be a helluva way to go.

. . . Assuming he survived the night.

Teeth chattering so hard that he feared biting his tongue, Everett hunkered down to wait. If he didn't survive, at least it had been a good ride.

He regretted not calling his parents before

heading out on this mission. He regretted not saving his best friend's son. Most of all, he regretted never having seen what he'd imagined to be his angel's long, blond hair . . .

Mary Margaret woke stiff and sore, but drenched in gentle morning sun.

The previous night rushed into her mind like a sudden wind gust, blustery and unwanted.

Everett Black was dead.

How could she miss a man she'd never even known? Yet she did. With a biting, keening intensity that made it hard to breathe past the knot in her throat.

She ducked her head, burying her face in the baby's downy hair.

For him, she had to stay strong. She had to uncover the Jeep, somehow drive it down from the rocky perch where Everett had left it, then make her way to America. The whole of which felt beyond impossible. She had to break it down. First creep from the vehicle to ensure none of Señora's men remained.

With the sleeping infant cradled to her chest, she nudged open the Jeep's passenger-side door. Upon hearing it groan in protest, she cringed. But when no one else seemed to have heard, she continued on.

Her most pressing issue was an urgent need of a restroom.

Nuns didn't typically mosey about the forest, let alone raise their skirts to relieve themselves outdoors, but Mary Margaret settled the baby on the still-warm seat, took wipes from his bag, then accomplished the first of what she could only imagine would be countless more steps toward acclimating herself toward a secular life.

Finished, she changed the baby's diaper, then crept to the edge of the rock that afforded her the best view of the road below. It was empty. No sign of any of the señora's men.

Exhaling in relief, she scooped up the baby, then gingerly maneuvered the hillside. Her long, wool skirt caught on countless vines and brambles, but a minute later, she'd made it to the muddy road, only to run across, catching herself twice when the slick surface threatened her balance.

She should be leaving this very second.

She was wasting valuable time in even looking at the grisly accident scene.

Only Everett Black's death had been no accident, but a sacrifice for her and his friends' son. For as long as she lived, she'd never forget his selfless act.

Tears streaming down her cheeks, she gathered

SHUNNED

her skirt to keep it from dragging in the mud, then
slowed when she reached the cliff's edge.

Holding tight to the baby, she peered over, soon
finding the charred remains of the convent van. By
now, the shame of what she'd done must be the talk
of everyone she knew. If only she could have trusted
them to share the real truth. Then maybe everything
would be different.

Mr. Black might still be alive.

She was turning away when the glint of sun on
metal caught her eye, and then she gasped, trembling
hands covering her mouth. *Mr. Black?*

Was he somehow alive?

Exhilaration swelled her chest.

Leaning further over the edge, she called, "Mr.
Black! Can you hear me?"

Her voice jolted him awake. His eyes opened,
then shut with a flutter. He raised his hands,
shielding them from the sun.

She winced to see his palms and fingertips
bloodied.

"Mr. Black? How can I help?"

"Give me a sec." He half waved. "I've got this."

"You're covered in blood, and your knee was
already hurt before you started. How you survived
the van going over the cliff is a miracle straight from
God above." Keeping a tight one-armed hold on the
baby, she made the sign of the cross.

"No kidding." He chuckled. "If lightning hadn't

shown me this ledge, I'd have been a goner, but—"

He'd rolled onto to one knee when a huge section of the ledge crumpled out from beneath him.

She screamed.

He released a string of curses.

And just when Mary Margaret thought their situation couldn't grow worse, her heart couldn't beat faster, from somewhere down the road came the sound of an approaching vehicle.

The señora and her men?

10

Jacksonville, Florida

"Judging by your expression," Nash said to Harding while pacing outside Maisey's ICU room, "I'm afraid to even ask what Briggs and Jasper reported."

"It isn't good." Harding cupped his hand to Nash's shoulder, giving it a squeeze. "Shit . . ." He bowed his head. "I don't even know how to say this—and hey, so far, our intel on this mission has been a straight-up cluster fuck, but—"

"Just say it!" Nash hadn't meant to snap, but his nerves were beyond frayed. It didn't matter that Joe wasn't biologically his, the love he felt for that baby and Maisey made him whole. Hell, he'd literally helped bring the little guy into the world. For him to be gone? Nash refused to believe it possible. Just like he knew Maisey had to wake soon, he chose to believe Joe and Everett would soon be found safe, as well. They had to.

The alternative was unthinkable.

"At 0735, Briggs and Jasper made contact with a local who reported a convent van had been stolen in the night by a gringo and nun. Might not be significant, but here's the kicker, the guy also reported that they're being accused of having stolen Señora Rodriguez's baby. Compounding the issue, storms in the area damaged the already sketchy mountain road. The van was found by Camilla Rodriguez's security team after having gone over the edge, where, upon landing, there was an explosion."

Lips pressed tight to prevent crying out, Nash squeezed his hands into fists. The emotional pain hurt far worse than anything physical he'd ever endured.

"But look, man . . ." Harding was back to squeezing his shoulder. "You and I both know Everett is the best. Who's to say he didn't stage the crash as a diversion?"

"You don't think Camilla's men would have checked?"

"Apparently, the van's wreckage is in too deep of a ravine to easily access. They're scrambling to find someone who can rappel to the site. Another point working in our favor? Everett's a freakin' monkey. If anyone can keep your son alive, it's him. So come on . . ." He turned him toward the ICU exit door. "Let me buy you a coffee and donut. Grab a pager from Olivia at the nurse's desk and she'll let you know the second Maisey wakes. And she will. *Believe.*"

Nash nodded.

He wanted to believe everything would work out in a unicorn-studded rainbow, but he'd used up an awful lot of luck in just saving Maisey and Joe from her psychopath ex. How much more luck could one small family be allotted?

Was this the point when their supply finally crapped out?

11

Piapoco, Colombia

"Run!" Everett commanded of his angel. The approaching vehicle was large enough and close enough for the entire cliff face to shudder.

"I can't leave you," she cried. "What if—"

"Go!"

She did. Thankfully.

Eyes closed, he envisioned Camilla Rodriguez being smart enough to bring in big equipment to haul up the van's wreckage. To make sure she hadn't been duped. When that happened, he couldn't be found just sitting here with his thumbs up his ass. But honestly? He wasn't sure what else to do.

The vehicle stopped.

SHUNNED

The acrid smell of diesel dropped to Everett's ledge.

Rapid-fire Spanish he couldn't comprehend.

One door creaked open, then two. The sound carried crystal clear on the still morning air.

More talking.

Options? If Everett went up, the black widow's greeting committee would nail him on sight. If he went down . . .

He glanced at his hands. His fingertips were a bloody mess. If his grip failed—well . . . Suffice to say, it was a long way down.

Leaning back against the stone wall of his new prison, Everett envisioned his angel, drawing strength from the satisfaction he'd feel when he somehow got her and Baby Joe safely out of here. And he would. Just as soon as he devised a solid plan that didn't involve him meeting his angel's former boss.

More back-and-forth arguing overhead, and then, *"Hola, Señor!"*

From Heaven, a rope fell, literally conking Everett on his thick head.

Are you shitting me? Had that vehicle belonged to good guys?

He couldn't help but smile. He was so happy his angel hadn't followed his directions that he could kiss her. But first, he'd once and for all slip off her nun's cap, letting the blond hair he'd imagined fall like a halo.

"*Senor! Agarrar la cuerda!*"

Everett had no idea what the grizzled old man had said, and he didn't much care. His wild gestures said it all—grab the rope. So he did.

Testing the sun-faded and frayed rope's hold, he gave it a tug and found it solid. After pulling himself upright, he aligned the rope with his good leg, then used a classic brake and squat technique for wrapping the rope around his foot to push off, then alternately pull himself up. His fingertips screamed with each upward lurch, but he maintained a solid pace for twenty vertical feet.

He looked up to find his angel holding the baby, peering over the ledge, smiling, motioning him higher. He barely even knew her, yet the curve of her lips spurred him on, faster and harder to reach her, to get her and Baby Joe safely back to the States where they could take their time getting to know each other in a setting that didn't involve a murdering, kidnapping, and a drug lord's widow.

Closing the gap between them, he ignored burning pain in favor of focusing on her blue eyes. They matched the sky. Would they lighten or darken with her moods? He'd like nothing more than to discover all of her moods at their leisure.

Up and up he climbed until sweat dripped from his forehead into his eyes.

By tonight, they'd have reached a town far

enough from Camilla's influence that they could share a steak dinner before arranging for transport home. By tonight, he'd have seen her blond hair. He'd have heard all of her story. He'd have bought her new clothes and be partway to convincing her that maybe a new life away from the convent might not be so bad . . .

With only five-feet to the go, the time-worn rope creaked, and then he dropped an inch when one of the strands popped. And then another and another so fast that he frantically searched for a handhold before—too late.

The rope broke, and he was no longer gazing into his angel's welcoming sky, but falling, falling into the black nothingness of his mortality.

Mary Margaret screamed. "*Nooooo!*"

He'd been so close to the top. *Why, God? Why would You cruelly let him almost reach safety only to let him fall?* To let all of us fall? For without him, any victory would only serve as a reminder of how much she'd already lost.

"Mr. Black? Everett? Can you hear me?" He'd thankfully landed back on the ledge where he'd started, but he wasn't moving. She pressed her hands to her chest, willing her heart to slow.

In her arms, the baby fitfully cried. She'd prayed that by the time he woke, she and Everett would be underway, safely en route to another town, another place far, far from the pain of this awful mountain.

The two locals she'd guessed to be coffee farmers by the sacks of beans in the truck bed, carried on an animated discussion with much gesturing back and forth between the truck and Everett and herself. Had they heard the señora's infant had been taken? If so, had they guessed she and Everett were to blame? Would the men keep their secret or were they paid too well by the señora?

Mary Margaret's stomach churned at the thought.

On the truck's grill was a winch spooled with cable.

The younger of the two men fished behind the passenger seat in the truck's cab to pull out a nylon rope that he looped around his waist, then knotted.

The white-haired man climbed behind the truck's wheel, then maneuvered the lumbering vehicle around so that the winch faced the cliff's edge. The sideways truck blocked the narrow road to oncoming traffic.

After affixing the cable's hooked end to his rope, he stood at the ready until the older man exited the truck to work the winch's controls.

All the while, the baby cried and Mary Margaret forgot to breathe.

SHUNNED

Even if these two saints got Everett up alive, how badly was he hurt? She would need to find him medical help—fast. But where? The nearest hospital was the convent, but obviously, she couldn't take him there.

Realizing that standing around fretting would get her nowhere, she lurched into action. A short march up the hill landed her at the Jeep where she used canned formula to prepare a bottle for the baby. While feeding him, she stood alongside the boulder, watching, waiting, holding her breath while the kindly old man worked the winch, shouting directions back and forth with his partner.

Time stretched into an impossibly long thread.

She paced, patting the baby's back, and when the tension grew to be too much for her to bear, she dragged the camouflage netting off of the Jeep, then rummaged through the back of the vehicle for makeshift infant car seat supplies. Spying a backpack, she dumped its contents, tucked the infant inside, then securely strapped him onto the Jeep's rear seat. It by no means was the perfect way to travel with an infant, but in this emergency situation, the temporary set-up would have to do.

With the baby safe, she checked the men and found them still working.

She did the same, searching for the Jeep's keys and finding them beneath the driver's seat just as Everett had said.

The day had already grown warm. After the previous night's rain, the air felt thick with humidity. As she climbed behind the Jeep's steering wheel, her habit's long skirt bunched about her ankles, making it hard to even see the pedals. After hiking the skirt up to her knees, she tucked the fabric beneath her. The air on her legs felt foreign and uncomfortable, yet at the same time, freeing.

The Jeep had an automatic transmission.

She fit the key into the ignition.

In case of an emergency, her father had taught her to drive an old Ford Explorer they'd used for supply runs. Her throat tightened at the memory of his patient smile. Over and over, he'd explained that she couldn't have her feet on the gas and brake pedals at the same time.

In an odd way, that's how she felt about the sudden changes in her life.

Part of her desperately missed the convent's peace and satisfying routine. Another part of her, the part disillusioned by the sisters' countless lies, longed to press her foot hard to the accelerator and travel as far from this place as the Jeep would take her.

She forced a deep breath, then settled her foot on the brake before starting the engine. Once it chugged with a satisfying rhythm, she squeezed her eyes shut for the briefest of moments, knowing that when she left the safety of this glade, her life would never be the same.

SHUNNED

Everett had backed in the vehicle, making her task in getting it to the road no big deal. All she had to do was place the gears in drive, then let gravity take over. The tricky part would be stopping before she drove right over the ledge like the convent van.

She accelerated just enough to drive the vehicle over a brush pile Everett must have created, then ever-so-gently accelerated down the hill.

Progress was slow and steady until her long, full skirt worked free, tangling between her ankles and the brake. Suddenly, the Jeep rolled faster and faster until hitting the road's squishy mud, then fishtailing.

She yanked the wheel as hard as she could to the left, but the mud sucked in the tires, taking the car where it wanted to go—straight toward the cliff.

12

Jacksonville, Florida

"Nash?" Maisey found it difficult to say even her husband's name. Her breathing tube had been removed and her throat ached and burned. But nothing could hurt worse than the knowledge that her son and now Everett were still missing and presumed dead.

"I'm right here, babe." Her husband had been dozing in an armchair beside her. Maisey's love for him was so much bigger and better than anything she'd ever prayed to find. Her love for her son? Somehow even more grand, because even though Nash wasn't Joe's biological father, the fact that he'd welcomed both her and her tiny son into his heart and soul had filled her to an indescribable degree.

Which was beautiful.

But also made their current situation all the more untenable.

Without her son, life felt impossible.

Hot, messy tears fell and refused to stop.

Nash silently rose, then lowered the rail on her hospital bed to gently draw her into his arms. "Everything's going to be all right."

"B-but what you said about the e-explosion, what—"

He drew back, framing her face with his big, strong hands. Meeting her tear-filled gaze he said, "I refuse to believe the worst, okay? Everett is one, tough S.O.B. If anyone can get our son safely home, it's him."

She nodded. Maisey wanted to believe her husband's words were true, but another part of her was terrified that this time Vicente Rodriguez might ultimately win—even from beyond the grave.

"I love you." Nash kissed her forehead and nose and finally, softly, her lips. "The doctor said you're getting stronger by the hour. At the rate you're improving, Nurse Olivia said they'll soon be moving you out of ICU. Which means that by the time Everett and Briggs and Jasper get back with Joe, you'll have ditched a bunch of these tubes and might even be home."

"B-but what if Camilla doesn't stop? What if we

get Joe back only to lose him again?"

"We'll cross that bridge when we get to it. All you need to worry about is getting better. Joe needs his mom." He kissed her. "I need my wife."

I need you.

What Maisey didn't need was to live the rest of her life fearing Camilla Rodriguez. The woman was even more insidious than her husband had been. And since she rarely left her compound, she'd be even more difficult to kill.

Maisey didn't like thinking of herself as being capable of taking a life, but when it came to protecting her husband and son, all bets were off . . .

13

Piapoco, Colombia

"Muchas gracious," everett had said to the man who'd saved his sorry ass. Unfortunately, his relief over finally returning to the muddy road was short lived.

Over the diesel truck's chugging idle rose another engine—this one, from the adjacent hillside. Still on his knees, it was then it occurred to him that his angel was missing. Had she taken it upon herself to not only coordinate a second rescue mission, but prep his Jeep for travel?

A glance in that direction had him grinning, but then cringing.

"Babe! You're taking that hill too—" There was

no time to finish his observation before she'd careened the Jeep onto the road's mud, then damn near decapitated him before finally stopping a scant three inches from the edge of the cliff it felt as if he'd spent three lifetimes climbing.

"You're safe!" Before Everett took his next breath, she'd hopped from behind the wheel, gingerly avoiding the ledge before running through the muck to him. Her once pristine habit hung from her too-thin frame in a depressing, mud-covered mass. Regardless, she was the most beautiful sight he'd ever seen. On her knees in front of him, she looked as if she might kiss him, but then, as if checking herself, she drew back.

"It's okay," he said with a lopsided smile. "Go for it."

"I don't know what you're talking about." Her darting gaze told a different story, but they could sort that out later. For now, it was time to get while for once, the getting was actually good.

The virile young man who'd saved him sported spiky hair and a Rolling Stones T-shirt. Through his bickering with the older guy with the wiry white hair and beard, Everett guessed they were grandson and grandfather. Through much painful handshaking, hugs, and relieved smiles, Everett hoped they understood how grateful he truly was.

He was also suspicious about why Camilla Rodriguez and her men hadn't yet returned. Surely, she was smarter than to take the wrecked van at face value. Could they really be so lucky as to have her permanently out of the picture?

Everett was skeptical, but not complaining.

"Hand over the keys," he said to his angel once the men climbed back into their truck.

"Not a chance," she said. "After what you've been through, you need rest and a bath—not necessarily in that order."

He laughed. He wasn't used to being around such a bossy, take-charge woman, but she was growing on him . . .

"Let me help you." He did, and by the time she assisted him in limping to the Jeep's passenger side, then opening his door, the relief of sitting on an actual padded seat shimmered through him. For the moment, life was good.

Wide-eyed, from his perch in a makeshift carrier, Baby Joe sucked on a mustache-style pacifier. The kid looked adorable, and Everett couldn't wait to tell Nash and Maisey the great news—that he was bringing their son safely home. Unfortunately, the black widow had long since taken his sat phone, so until reaching civilization, he had no way of letting them know.

"Thanks," Everett said when his angel buckled his seat belt, then checked the baby in his makeshift carrier before rounding the Jeep to climb behind the wheel. "For everything. There's no way I could have pulled this off without you."

"While I appreciate your gratitude, I owe you thanks, as well." She put the vehicle in drive, then once again tucked her long skirt before carefully proceeding down the mountain. "You opened my eyes to an entire world I'd never seen."

"How so?" He angled to better face her.

"In every way possible. Remember how I told you I'd been repeatedly denied the privilege of taking my final vows?"

"Yeah . . ."

"One of my favorite sisters basically accused me of being naïve, and she was right. I have no proof, but I think in an indirect way, Señora Rodriguez was responsible for killing my parents. And yet all this time, I stayed at the convent, helping in her ministry. Yet what kind of good deeds are funded by cocaine's evil? It's sick. And I blindly, stupidly lived my life believing everything anyone ever said. I'm an idiot." Taking one hand off the wheel, she tore at the pins holding her wimple and veil in place.

"Stop beating yourself up. From what you told me, you were basically still a kid when your folks were killed. How could you have possibly known what was going on? From the outside, it seemed like a pretty nice place."

She snorted, then pitched one, two, three, four bobby pins to the floorboard.

Everett held his breath, anticipating his first

sight of her long blond hair. How odd was it that he felt as if he knew her on an intimate level, yet he'd never even seen her hair? Had only imagined it?

Hand at the top of her head, she removed her fabric crown.

He'd expected to be blown away by her ethereal beauty, but the reality of her full appearance must have registered as shock.

She took one look at him, stupidly gaping at her, then burst into tears. "Not only am I stupid, but ugly, right? Sister Agnes said long hair is a vanity. A sin. Each month, we took turns cutting each other's hair with kitchen scissors."

"You're stunning." And now that he'd had a minute to work through his initial surprise, he reached out, stroking her dark pixie cut, loving its softness against his rock-roughened fingertips and palms.

Both hands back on the wheel, she leaned into his touch. Tears still shone in her big blue eyes. If there was no urgent need to put as many miles as possible between themselves and Camilla, he'd have told his angel to pull over. He had the craziest urge to draw her onto his lap and kiss her until she actually believed how lovely she truly was—inside and out.

They drove in silence for hours, eventually stopping at a shack that had an enormous fuel tank alongside it that sat on stilts. Everett had stashed a couple million in Colombian pesos in various hidey holes throughout the Jeep. A fact that came in handy with gasoline costing a whopping nine thousand pesos per gallon. After paying the clerk an extra couple thousand to let them use a water hose to wash their hands and faces, Everett also shelled out another three thousand for bread and local goat cheese.

He added another wad of bills to bribe the owner to forget they were there.

They'd made so many twists and turns on their journey, paying off locals along the way, that by the time Camilla realized she'd been duped, Everett prayed they had at least several hours of lead time on her thugs. He was under no illusion that they'd escaped home free. It was only a matter of time before they encountered the señora and her hired guns again.

"Your hands look horrible," his angel noted. She held the baby, bouncing him while he grabbed for an iridescent blue butterfly. "I'm guessing we'll reach Medellin within a few hours. We'll be able to buy medical supplies there."

He waved off her concern. "As soon as we find a phone, we're golden. I'll get in touch with my team lead, and he'll send help. In fact, since I was supposed to have called in a couple days ago, I wouldn't be surprised if guys from my company are already in country."

"Your team? Company?" She'd arched her head back as if drinking in sun. Light perspiration coated her pale skin, making her look every bit the angel he'd imagined her to be. Since she was no longer an official nun, once he got her safely back on US soil, he'd ask her out on an official date. "Does that mean there are more of you crazy commando types, roaming the Colombian jungle?"

"I guess you could say that. We work for a security team. It's based out of Denver, but we have guys set up all over the US."

"Like bodyguards?"

"Sure—only usually more intense. High-profile cases pay the bills, but we still have time to help people who have nowhere else to turn."

She nodded, and side-by-side, they walked as fast as his bum knee allowed back to the Jeep.

"If this is too personal," he said, "feel free to tell me to mind my own business, but when was the last time the top of your bare head felt sun?"

"Too long . . ." She rolled up her voluminous sleeves, but by the time they reached their ride, they'd fallen.

"Are you hot?" he asked. According to the Jeep's dash, the temp was only ninety-three, but the humidity wasn't doing them any favors. The gasoline's smell hung heavy in the still air.

"Very."

He opened the glove box for a pocket knife. "If

you're sure about giving up on the church, it would just take a sec for me to modify your habit. Might make you more comfortable in this heat."

She glanced at the hardscrabble ground, then back to him. Worrying her full lower lip, she nodded. "Please, have your way with me."

Clearly, she had no clue what she'd just said. Or maybe he just had a dirty mind. Either way, he opened his knife, then grabbed hold of the seam between her shoulder and the sleeve. "You're sure?"

Her faint smile and nod did the funniest things to his normally calm stomach, and when he worked the knife into the seam, prying the threads apart, baring her creamy white skin, he was forced to shift his weight to hide his erection. The innocent had no idea what she did to him. Probably just as well, considering his no-commitment rule.

With one sleeve worked free, he handed her the fabric, then started on the other side.

A happy sigh escaped her lips. "Sister Agnes would have a cow if she caught me like this." She waved her freed limb as if she were a butterfly emerging from her cocoon. "But I guess it doesn't matter now."

"Once we get back to the States, what are you going to do?" He was trying to play it cool. Not to act as if he'd never seen a woman's bared arms before. But the funny thing was, he'd never seen any of her. No one had. Which made her shiny and new.

"I have no idea."

When the gas pump attendant appreciatively eyed her, Everett practically growled.

"Ready?" he asked upon completing his task.

"Yes." She cast a worried glance over her shoulder. "But I can't shake the feeling that things have been going a little too smoothly ever since we got off of that mountain."

"True."

She tucked Baby Joe back into his pack, then asked, "Do you think there's a chance Señora Rodriguez really thinks we're all dead?"

He shrugged. "My gut says no. But if that is the case, why not send an army of her goons out after us?"

"Great question.

14

Jacksonville, Florida

"The doctor said you can go home soon." Nash set Maisey's favorite cashew chicken takeout on her hospital tray. Her color was almost back to normal. Her bruised arms only sported one IV. Her forehead and cheeks were still swollen and green from her beating, but her indomitable resolve to get back their son had her in rare fighting form.

"I want to go now." She pushed the tray away. "I can't stand not knowing where my baby is."

"I told you, Briggs and Jasper learned without a doubt that two coffee farmers helped a man up from a rock ledge. A nun with a baby waved them down for help. As soon as Everett is able, he'll check in, and then Briggs and Jasper will bring all three of them home."

"Who is this nun? What if she can't be trusted?"

"Hon . . ." Nash crossed his arms. "If you don't relax, I'm going to call for Nurse Olivia to come in here and give you a shot of something that makes you a little less salty to the man who loves you." He leaned across the bed to steal a kiss, starting off casual, but then deepening it for a bit of tongue. Knowing for an absolute certainty that their son and friend were safe, that his wife was on her way to a full recovery, had changed everything.

For the first time since this madness started, Nash felt as if he could finally exhale. Which led to one question—if he felt so good, why was his wife still feeling bad? Was his gut missing something?

Was Camilla Rodriguez only quiet, because she was already planning her next move?

15

Medellin, Colombia

When a knock sounded on the hotel room's door—they'd checked in under assumed names—Mary Margaret's pulse took off on the same runaway gallop it had when escaping the convent. The longer she and Everett had gone without incident, though, the more she dared hope their fear of being chased by bad guys was well and truly behind them.

A quick peek through the peephole showed Everett making a silly face.

She laughed, surprising even herself by her uncharacteristically high spirits.

After turning the deadbolt and unhooking a

chain lock, she opened the door to him. "I was starting to worry."

"Sorry. I wanted to find just the right things—for both of you." He brushed past her with several bags, overwhelming her with his delicious citrus and leather scent. He'd not only showered and shaved, but apparently found aftershave, as well. He'd called his teammates who were flying in from Bogotá, and would be there in the morning to chopper them back to the capital city where they'd then board a private jet. Everett had explained that reentering the States would be less messy for her that way.

Once they'd returned Baby Joe to his parents, Everett promised to help her reestablish her citizenship and forge a new life. He'd even been to a doctor for steroid shots to his knee. The wounds on his fingertips were already healing and for the first time in her entire life, Mary Margaret was looking forward to sharing dinner with a man. "How is the little bugger?"

"See for yourself . . ." She pointed toward the room's king-sized bed where she'd made a pen for him with pillows. The cherub had drank a full bottle and was now napping. "My fingers are crossed for him to be just as peaceful during our dinner."

"Me, too." Everett set the bags atop a low dresser. "Well . . ." He shoved his hands in the pockets of his new khakis. "If you want to go ahead and shower and change, I'll watch the baby."

"O-okay." Call her a prude, but Mary Margaret felt they didn't know each other well enough to share a room. But for safety, Everett had insisted. She should have stood her moral ground, but what was the point when she'd have only added to her sins of new lust by lying? "Thank you, Mr. Garcia."

"You're welcome, Mrs. Garcia." The thrill of being with him, pretending to be his wife, in this relatively large city had excitement bubbling through her as if her blood had somehow turned to champagne. All of her worry and fear dissolved, making way for the intoxicating thrill of her first crush—something she'd never in a million years planned, yet here she was, loving every minute of it.

Sister Catherine had been right.

Mary Margaret had been naïve. Had she taken her final vows to God, she wouldn't now be poised on the brink of a sparkly new life—which would officially start with her first bath in nearly two decades.

Before she went and did something stupid like actually giggling, she snatched up the bags Everett had brought her, then scurried into the restroom. After closing and locking the door, she leaned hard against it, dropping the bags to press her palms to her fevered cheeks. The notion that she'd soon be naked mere feet from where Everett had stretched across the bed . . .

She fanned herself, then crossed the room to

turn on the bathtub's faucets.

The convent didn't have a tub—showers were seen as luxuries and only allowed twice a week for a strict five minutes.

Mary Margaret recalled her mother buying her bubble bath for birthdays and Christmas, so she poured some of the rose-scented hotel shampoo into her running water.

While waiting for the tub to fill, she dove into Everett's packages. There were capri pants and silky blouses in a rainbow of colors. Dresses and headscarves and even lacy undergarments.

The thought of him selecting, let alone touching such private things had more heat rising on her cheeks. He'd thought of everything—even light cotton pajamas and strappy sandals in white, silver, and pink.

The last bag contained clothes for the baby. Adorable onesies in blue, red, and green. Also, tiny blue plaid pants and a white shirt. The outfit would be perfect for when Baby Joe was reunited with his mother and father. Everett had even found itty bitty socks and shoes. The man really had thought of everything.

A splashing sound sent her gaze skittering in that direction. She laughed to find bubbles having overflowed onto the floor.

"Sister Agnes would not be amused," she said in an exaggerated harsh tone before laughing while turning off the water, then removing her habit for what would be the last time.

There were no mirrors in the convent—vanity was a sin.

Appraising herself for the first time as a woman, let alone a fully nude woman, in the floor-to-ceiling mirror came as a shock. So much had changed. She gingerly touched her breasts, surprised when her nipples hardened.

Ashamed, she covered them with her palms, but that only worsened her condition. Was there something wrong? And what was that strange hum between her legs? She squeezed her thighs tighter, but that only worsened the problem.

Sex was *never* discussed at the convent.

Mary Margaret's parents had passed long before it would have even been appropriate for them to have given her *the talk*.

She never thought sex would be an issue, so she'd never given it much thought. But now, after spending so much time with Everett, maybe she should? Not have sex. But at least try finding out more about it? Once she returned to America, surely any library would have books about it?

She skimmed her hand across her flat abdomen, lower to pat the springy hair crowning the vee between her legs. And then her gaze dropped to the hair growing on her thighs and calves. On the drive into town—even on market days with the sisters—

she'd noted that secular women shaved their legs and armpits. Sister Agnes categorized shaving as a sin, so that had also been forbidden. Since Mary Margaret had never bared her legs or armpits, the issue had never mattered, but considering the clothes Everett had brought, her hairiness was now a huge issue.

Thankfully, she recalled her mother shaving, but since Everett wouldn't let her leave the room, and even if she did, she had no money, then how would she get her hands on shaving cream and a razor?

Did she dare ask Everett to bring both items?

Depends.

Which would be a bigger embarrassment? Admitting to him she needed help? Or showing up with him at a restaurant while looking like a hairy freak?

Worrying her lower lip, she eyed a fluffy white robe hanging from the back of the bathroom door, then made a risqué decision . . .

16

Everett stood outside of the hotel room's bathroom door, sweating as if he were drenched in midday sun. His angel had asked for help, and he'd give it. After what they'd been through, he'd give her anything—do anything to help her transition into her new life.

But doing so might just be the death of him.

He'd never met anyone quite like her.

It was as if she'd stepped out of another time. She was unspoiled in every way, and because of this, he felt honor-bound to respect her in every way.

Upon finally summoning the courage to knock, she answered in a breathless rush—almost as if she was as apprehensive about this seemingly simple act as he was. "You're back. Thank you."

She'd changed into one of the hotel's white robes. It showed the pale vee of her throat, as well as the calves she was so concerned about.

"I, ah, grabbed everything I thought you may need, plus a bathing suit." Determined to handle this in a clinical manner, Everett cleared his throat and held out another bag, this one from the lobby gift shop. "That way, if you need help, I can be in the bathroom with you, but you're still . . ." he gestured up and down his chest, hoping he wasn't as red-faced as he feared, ". . . you know."

She nodded and snatched the bag from him. "Thank you. Please watch Baby Joe while I change."

Everett perched on the foot of the bed and gulped.

He was in way over his head on this one. His body craved things he had no right to ask—things his angel might never feel ready to give. And that was okay—probably even for the best. He had that rule about no-commitment and this saint deserved a ring, white picket fence, and the kind of lifelong promise he might never be able to give.

It was with all of that in mind that when she opened the bathroom door and stepped out in the most chaste, white one-piece he'd been able to find, that he gulped, then rapidly looked away. "Great. I'm glad it fits. Now, you can get started."

"By myself?" She looked confused.

"Sure. Go ahead and try everything out. I'll stay

out here with Baby Joe. Call me if you need back-up."

Since the baby was sleeping, Everett flipped through a tourism brochure he'd found near the TV. Oddly enough, every picture featured one of his imagined images of his angel.

"Everett?" she called from the bathroom.

"Yeah?" He loved hearing her say his name. What was wrong with him that he found the sound so pleasurable passing her lips?

"I think I already messed this up. Would you mind helping?"

"Not at all." He stood ramrod straight, willing away his erection. He took a few deep breaths, thinking of that time way back in basic training when he'd accidentally seen his chubby drill sergeant wearing only his skivvies. There. That worked. At least until he entered the cramped bathroom to find his angel perched on the side of the tub.

At his angle, the mounds of her perfect, creamy breasts were all too visible. The kissable back of her neck. The womanly swell of her hips that he'd hold while sinking himself—no.

Clinical, man. This is a clinical operation.

He saw right away what her problem was, and he knelt on the cold tile floor beside the tub. The pose hurt like the devil, but in this case, physical pain was exactly what he needed to get his mind off of other more pressing regions. She'd spread at least half the can of mango-scented shaving cream over her calf and shin, meaning the foam was so thick that the razor stood zero chance of landing on any hair.

"What did I do wrong?" she asked, eyebrows knitting with concern.

"I'm no expert, but . . ." Using the edge of his palm as a spatula, he wiped away most of the foam. "I'm guessing you used a little too much of this." He took the razor from her, gliding it over her shin. Once the blade was filled, he leaned to the sink, notched up the single lever faucet, then rinsed the razor beneath the water's flow. Might not be environmentally cool, but he left the tap running, repeating the process again and again until her right leg was irresistibly smooth. He couldn't help himself from skimming his palm along the curve of her slender calf, greedily wanting to glide higher.

He'd worked up to about mid-thigh on that leg before she covered his hand with hers. Her breathing fell in soft, breathy hitches. Her pupils were wide.

She licked her lips. "I-I think I can handle it from here."

"Sure?" He couldn't move his hand from her inner thigh. Didn't want to.

She shook her head, then nodded.

He somehow found the strength to release her, then pass the razor. "Need anything else?"

"No, thank you." She pressed her free hand to her chest. "I'm good."

"I'm glad." He pushed himself up, gritting through knee pain so as not to look like a weaker man than she deserved. He found himself wanting to be everything for her. Her knight in shining armor. Might sound corny, but he didn't care. Something about her attracted him like a magnet. When push came to shove, her softness was contrasted by an equally capable tough side. Part of him wanted to say, screw his no-commitment rule and downright woo her with every trick in his pathetic playbook. On the other hand, he feared she was too good for him, so why even try? "Sure you won't hurt yourself?"

"Positive." She held her hand over the spot on her inner thigh where his hand had just been. Could she still feel his touch the way he felt her?

He forced himself to turn away, then closed the bathroom door behind him.

Once Everett left the perilously small space, Mary Margaret missed him almost as much as she feared him—not in a safety sort of way. More like the crazy, topsy-turvy way he made her feel. The way her heart uncomfortably thumped. Not from fright, but heightened awareness.

She now fully understood why Sister Agnes had believed that it was a sin for a woman to shave her legs. Because of how good a man's hands felt skimming across that smooth skin.

Mary Margaret finished her task, then rinsed the tub, dried off, and luxuriated in coating herself with the hotel-provided lotion. It smelled of gardenias. And it too was most likely a sin. But Mary Margaret had stopped caring. What the sisters had done to her in keeping the señora's dark secrets had also been a sin. A sin much worse than the supposed wickedness of touch.

She slipped on her new lacy panties and bra, only to discover more frustration. The unfamiliar fabric kissed her most private places in a provocative way. Much different from her standard-issue white cotton. Next, she pulled on a full-skirted dress constructed of a soft fabric that matched her eyes.

When she peered in the mirror, she didn't know the woman staring back at her. The image of herself she remembered was that of a frightened child. She was now a woman. Her cheeks superheated at the mere thought of all the things secular women were allowed to do.

Would she ever feel comfortable in her own skin? For now, the answer eluded her. But maybe someday soon, Everett might be so kind as to help her figure it out?

Ten minutes later, with Everett carrying the baby, the three of them walked to a restaurant near the hotel. Night had fallen. Heat rose from the dirty pavement. The streets were packed with what she could only call partiers. Men and women in all manner of dress and levels of intoxication. Neon lights blinked and glared. Smells accosted her—some pleasant, like grilled meat. Some not, like stale urine. As optimistic as she'd been in her room's relative safety, she now felt out of her element and unsure.

She found herself practically clinging to Everett, and when they stopped on a corner to wait for traffic to stop long enough for them to cross, he asked, "You okay?"

"I'm sorry, but no. Would you mind finding something to eat closer to the hotel?"

"All you had to do was ask." He hailed a taxi, and five minutes later, paid the driver, then helped her into their hotel's air-conditioned, marble-floored lobby.

Baby Joe had grown fussy.

She jiggled him in an attempt to calm him.

Everett placed his hand on the small of her back, guiding her toward a long hall crowned by glittering crystal chandeliers. Their footfalls were silent on a creamy confection of carpet spun with gold fibers. At the hall's end were double doors flanked by enormous potted palms.

SHUNNED

"My apologies, but this is a private party." A bearded man dressed in a dark suit blocked their path. He carried a clipboard.

"Wait here," Everett whispered into her ear. The warmth of his breath made her shiver.

He approached the man, exchanged words, passed him a wad of bills, and then gestured for her to approach.

Moments later, they shared a cozy booth. One waiter brought Baby Joe a high chair. Another waiter brought garlic butter and French bread, still warm from the oven.

A pianist played classical music on a low stage.

Elegantly dressed diners filling the room reminded Mary Margaret of some of the señora's formal affairs.

"What did you say to that man?" Mary Margaret was almost afraid to ask.

"I told him my wife and child were exhausted from traveling all day, and that if he'd kindly allow us to share a quick meal, he would be well compensated. I handed him an obscene amount of cash and voila—here we sit."

"Your wife? Your child?" Despite her heart having skipped a delicious beat at the mere notion, she raised her eyebrows.

"Would that be so horrible? Not right away, but maybe sometime down the road? After we get to know each other a little better?"

"Would you want kids?"

"Very much." He skimmed his hand over the crown of Baby Joe's downy-covered head. "But I guess I've never thought much about it till now. You?"

Gaze blurred with tears, she said, "I don't know. All of this is so new. I feel reborn. I'm afraid it's going to take me a while to adjust. Caring for myself is overwhelming enough. I can't imagine having my own child to look after as well."

She looked to Everett to find his expression strangely sad. Why?

How long would it be until she understood his moods as well as those of her fellow sisters'? Would she ever? What if once they returned to the States, they never saw each other again? What if he'd rather be with a woman who knew how to shave her legs and kiss and wear normal clothes? What if he tired of having to teach her everything from scratch?

That very real possibility stole her appetite.

The first waiter reappeared and Everett ordered a steak, while she made do with a bowl of steaming minestrone.

The simple dish reminded her of the last time she'd helped Sister Catherine in her kitchen. Would she ever see her again? A fierce, unexpected pang to hug her old friend caught her off guard. In leaving the convent, what had she done? Of course, helping Everett had been the right thing, but at what cost?

Was she fooling herself to ever believe she'd forge a new life that was even half as satisfying as what she'd had at the convent? Maybe she'd liked being naïve. It was certainly a whole lot easier than dealing with this new constant barrage of sights and sounds and smells and, most especially, emotions.

There was one thing that terrified Mary Margaret far more than Señora Rodriguez's guards...

Her budding feelings for Everett.

Her fear that those feelings might never be returned.

What if Everett thought her pathetic? Too afraid of her own shadow to walk down a crowded nighttime street. Moreover, how would she cope with not only never seeing her fellow beloved sisters again, but possibly him, too?

"You're awfully quiet," he said.

She cast him a faint smile. "It's been a long day."

"True." He bowed his head. "But are you sure that's it?"

Was this her perfect chance to at least try explaining emotions she didn't yet fully understand?

He reached toward her, almost as if he intended to hold her hands, but then the baby fussed, and she turned her attentions to the cranky munchkin beside her.

"He's probably exhausted."

"Sure." After slapping his napkin on the table, he asked, "Ready to head up?"

Mary Margaret nodded and opened her mouth to speak when the waiter appeared.

Without a sound, he handed Everett a note.

While reading, Everett's eyebrows furrowed. His formerly pleasant expression turned into a thin-lipped frown. How odd. What could the note say?

She didn't have long to wait. A moment later, he passed it to her.

YOU ARE SURROUNDED.
DO NOT TRY TO RUN OR CREATE A SCENE.
COME WITH ME PEACEABLY, AND NO ONE WILL BE HURT.

Mary Margaret dropped the note as if it had caught fire. Her heart rate surged while cupping her hand protectively to the back of the baby's head. She'd known this momentary lull was too good to be true. The señora had found them. There was nowhere left to hide.

She looked up, only to wish she hadn't.

Beneath a silver tray the waiter carried, he'd concealed a gun that was now aimed at her head.

17

*S*hit . . .

For Everett, seeing a gun aimed at the woman who trusted him to protect her evoked a visceral, even primal rage. No. On his watch, no harm would come to her or the baby. It was a no-brainer that eventually, Camilla's thugs would catch up with them, but Everett had hoped for at least a little more time. But no worries.

He forced a deep breath, calming his erratic pulse and fury.

While shopping for Mary Margaret's shaving supplies, he'd scouted the hotel's exits. From the booth, their safest bet would be ditching the gunman, then hustling through the kitchen to the loading dock. It would take thirty seconds tops.

Only problem with that plan? Odds were that this guy's friends waited for him just beyond the kitchen door. No bueno. Which meant going for Option B, which was essentially banking on the fact that by using a note, Camilla had tipped her hand that she was no more interested in making a scene than Everett was.

All he had to do was ditch Camilla's thug, then calmly guide Mary Margaret and the baby through the restaurant's main door and right back out to the lobby. Sounded easy enough in his head. But with both plans, there were too many variables.

The longer the gun stayed on Mary Margaret, the more Everett knew he was out of time. His heart hammered loud enough for him to hear in his ears.

Keep it cool, man. Pretend this is like any other mission.

Only it wasn't, because from out of nowhere, whatever it was he felt for the former nun, slugged him in his gut. He *had* to save her and the baby. Selfishly, he couldn't imagine his life without either of them.

Which was why he had to act now.

"Kindly tell your boss," Everett cleared his throat before setting the note back onto the waiter's tray, "that I prefer doing business face to face."

With the waiter momentarily distracted by looking at his tray, Everett grabbed his steak knife, then rammed it deep into the guy's family jewels.

The waiter cried out, dropping his tray and weapon.

The woman at the next table screamed.

"Come on," Everett knelt for the gun, ignoring the pain in his knee. "I'll take the baby. Let's head for the lobby."

"But that man can't have been alone." She struggled to her feet. "What if we run into his friends?"

"It's a chance we'll have to take." Everett scooped the baby from his high chair, then realized he couldn't very well provide cover while cradling an infant. "On second thought, you take Baby Joe. I need my hands free to shoot bad guys."

She took the baby.

Everett planted his hand against the small of her back, propelling her past panicked diners. In seconds the mood in the elegant room had gone from calm to chaos, with everyone now charging for the door.

Everett held Mary Margaret behind. "Let's let this mob work in our favor."

"How?" She was crying, hugging the baby to her chest.

"See that door just past the gift shop?"

She nodded.

"It leads to the—"

"Not so fast," a man said from behind them in broken English. "Give me the infant and I will let you and the woman go."

"Look away," Everett said to Mary Margaret.

He didn't have time to check if she'd complied. This was more of a shoot first, ask questions later, situation. Without a second thought, he shot the man in the chest and kept on walking.

The direct hit to his heart dropped the guy to the wood floor.

"Is he dead?" Mary Margaret's voice was barely audible over the restaurant patrons' screams.

"Hope so." He took her hand, dragging her in a zigzag pattern through the crowd.

Upon reaching the door opposite the gift shop, he pushed through first, checking that the coast was clear.

A short jog down a narrow corridor led them into a barely lit courtyard. Darkness sweetened by unseen flowers. The pool glowed like a sapphire. Crickets chirped.

"Think we're alone?" Mary Margaret asked.

"I wouldn't bet my life on it. Let's hurry to that access door on the other side." He pointed to an entrance flanked by towel carts. He'd have missed it were it not for the single bulb wall sconce mounted alongside it. "I don't want us exposed a second longer than necessary."

"Are we going back to our room?"

"No."

"Why? What about our stuff?"

"I've got a safe house not too far from here. It's already stocked."

"But how—"

"Look—" When the door they'd just come through opened, he pushed her into the shadows between two tall bushes. "If you could hold all questions for later, and trust that I've got this handled, we'd get you and the baby to safety a whole lot faster."

"W-what about you?"

"What do you mean?" His gaze narrowed. In the low light, it was tough making out her features. But it didn't matter, his heart knew every nuance from the tip of her slim nose to the blush of her high-boned cheeks.

"You need to be safe, too. I—we—need you."

His spirits soared. She needed him? *Nice.*

From out of the darkness came the sound of casual whistling, then a male voice calling, "Little mouse, little mouse, why won't you come out of your house?"

"Why won't they leave us alone?" Mary Margaret whispered.

"Stay here. No matter what happens, don't move."

"But—" Before she launched a protest, he was gone.

Keeping to the shadows, Everett crept around the courtyard's edge. The pool was rimmed with lounge chairs, which he stayed behind.

The whistling man was bold enough to now stand alongside the diving board. Shimmering light bathed his face in eerie blue. "You know I'll find you. Why not do us both a favor and hand over the infant?"

Everett pushed himself faster, while maintaining his stealth.

The courtyard was a long rectangle, and he was now in the cover of a small tiki-style bar. He took a moment to exhale the breath he'd been holding. He could shoot the whistling man, but not knowing how many more of Camilla's guys were in the hotel, he couldn't risk drawing attention.

Laughter sounded at the courtyard's opposite end.

Emerging from the door near Mary Margaret's hiding spot were a group of six twenty-somethings. Four guys and two girls. *Swell.* Just what he needed—more possibility of collateral damage.

Everett waited, hoping they were just passing through, but then they stopped by an umbrella-covered table. Two men sat, removing cigarettes from their shirt pockets. Their faces glowed while sharing a lighter. The acrid smell of smoke drifted on the calm night air.

The whistling man backed into a chair behind the diving board. Cloaked in shadows, no one besides Everett and Mary Margaret knew he was there.

The girls giggled while stripping down to their birthday suits.

Their companions did the same.

The naked foursome joined hands while running to the pool. They jumped in tandem, raising an epic splash.

Everett used the commotion to his advantage, leaving the bar's cover to venture closer to the man who had become his prey. Inch-by-inch, he crept along the tall, boxwood hedge. The palms of his hands still hurt from his climbing disaster, and each time they bumped against the leaves, it stung. But that was good. He needed the reminder of just how bad this situation could go. As long as Mary Margaret kept the baby quiet, there should be no issue with taking this guy down.

Just a few more feet . . .

The night was warm. Sweat popped out on his forehead. He wiped it with his forearm, then steadied himself for a final lunge.

Waaaahuh . . .

When the baby increased the volume of his cries, Everett froze.

18

Mary margaret hugged the infant to her chest, willing him to be quiet, but the poor thing cried loud enough to draw attention from not only the señora's hired gun, but the young people frolicking in the pool.

Moments earlier, she'd been shocked by their nudity, then envious of their apparent ease of their bodies.

Now, all she could selfishly think as the whistling man rose, then casually strolled toward her, was that she didn't want to die a virgin. Shame mixed with terror. She should fight, but how? With what? A branch?

Her mouth went dry with terror while her heart beat uncomfortably hard.

SHUNNED

The man came closer, and closer . . .

She closed her eyes. *This is it. He's going to take the baby and I'm going to die without ever having loved or even truly lived.*

Closer . . .

The men and women in the pool were now staring.

She couldn't go out like this. She might be a lot of things, but a coward wasn't one. After forcing a deep breath, Mary Margaret summoned every ounce of courage to charge at the man, hoping to knock him off balance. But turns out she needn't have bothered.

Just as she left her cover, he collapsed face down in front of her. A knife stuck out of his back.

She opened her mouth to scream, but then clamped her free hand over her mouth. Lord knew, the baby was doing a good enough job of drawing unwanted attention.

Everett stepped from the shadows, kneeling to jerk the blade from the deathly still man. He wiped off the excess blood on the man's suit sleeve.

"*¡Oye!*" One of the men from the pool swam to the edge. "*¿Necesita ayuda?*"

Everett started to answer, but Mary Margaret cut him off, replying in Spanish that no, the man didn't need help, but had drank too much tequila with dinner. They were going to get his wife.

The man smiled and nodded.

"Quick thinking," Everett whispered into her ear while easing his arm around her waist. "Let's get out of here."

He guided her through a door at the pool's far end, then down what felt like an endless corridor. He punched open a door marked, *Salida*, and they were once again outside, only this time onto a bustling street.

The contrast from hearing only the baby crying and the pounding of her own heart and running footfalls hit her like a slap. All of the sudden there was frenetic Latin music with a throbbing base. Blinding headlights and angry red taillights.

Everett flagged a cab, helped her and the baby into the backseat, handed the driver a card with an address, and then joined her before closing the door.

The sedan's windows were down, and the air smelled of exhaust and too many different foods. She felt sticky with sweat and afraid. But then Everett took her free hand, easing his fingers between hers.

"You did good back there. Real good."

"I was so scared." The words fell from her in a gush.

"Me, too." He raised her hand to his mouth, kissing the back. A thrill shivered through her. Suddenly, she wasn't so much scared, as exhilarated. They made a great team. Did he think so, too?

"I didn't think anything scared you."

He snorted, then skimmed the back of the still huffing baby's head. "When Baby Joe cried, and I saw that thug getting closer to the two of you, I literally thought my heart would beat out of my chest."

"Oh?" She licked her lips. A man had died back there, but she didn't care. He could very well have been one of the men who'd killed her parents. She had no pity for him. Let those who lived by the sword, die by the sword.

"I guess until just then, I didn't realize how much you two have come to mean. You're growing on me."

"Thank you." She was glad for the darkness, so he couldn't see her blush. "I feel the same—I mean, you're a good friend." Had she imagined it, or when she'd said *friend*, had he frowned?

Didn't he want that? Or did she dare hope that even in the short time they'd known one another, like her, he craved an indecipherable something more?

"It's not much," Everett said upon closing the door behind them in the safe house. "But it's clean, and no one should bother us."

"What about supplies for the baby?" Mary

Margaret's gaze darted about the spare space. It was a studio apartment on the fourth floor of an unremarkable walk-up. The only furniture was a bed, sofa, and table for the efficiency kitchen. Heavy drapes were drawn on four windows. Faint light shown from beyond the cracked door of what she assumed was a bathroom.

A window air conditioner unit hummed.

She shivered from the sudden chill.

"There should be plenty. I called ahead to have my associates stock the place with diapers and food and other baby stuff. There are also clothes for both of us, and a few snacks."

"You thought of everything."

"It's no biggie." He shrugged. "Just part of the job."

As it had back at their hotel, the thought of sharing the same room with him while they both slept felt wicked, as if she were caught by Sister Agnes, she'd be punished with weeks of extra kitchen duty. In the same breath, she wanted to be with him—not just for tonight, but always. Even in the most chaotic of times, he made her feel safe. That safety had become like a drug. She needed him. And considering the fact that as soon as they dropped the baby with his parents, they'd most likely never see each other again, that need was a problem.

He asked, "Want me to watch the baby while you grab a quick shower? All the excitement left me feeling sticky. I'll take one after you."

Two washings in one day? That kind of water usage was positively decadent, but she wasn't complaining.

She smiled and agreed.

He opened a closet and took a small suitcase from the floor. He set it on the sofa, unzipping it to show her silky PJs, slippers, and an assortment of light cotton clothes, shoes, and lacy pastel undergarments.

She gathered what she'd need, then darted off to the shower.

Beneath the hot spray, she tried pretending Everett wasn't just beyond the closed bathroom door. At the convent, her nakedness had always been a source of shame, but tonight, in the pool, those young women had seemed to celebrate the beauty of their nude bodies.

If Everett saw her, would he find her lacking?

At the moment of what she'd believed to be her certain death, the one thing she'd been most sorry about was dying a virgin. In hindsight, such a thought had been beyond sinful, but why? Why shouldn't she want to use her body in the way God had intended? As long as she loved the man she gave herself to, she failed to see the problem.

Does that mean I love Everett?

She pressed her hands to flaming cheeks that had turned hotter than the water. Maybe she did love him. And if this was to be the first and last night she ever spent with him, then she selfishly wanted more of their relationship. She wanted to know him in every way a woman could. She'd ask for forgiveness later, but now, with her pulse pounding harder than it ever had when faced by the señora's men, Mary Margaret turned off the taps, dried herself, then wrapped the towel around her before eking open the door.

She saw Everett stretched across the sofa.

The room was dark save for the flicker of a news broadcast playing on TV.

Baby Joe had curled onto his tummy in the crib.

Now that she'd started her crazy plan, Mary Margaret wasn't so sure this was a bright idea. What if Everett turned her down? How would she even know if she was doing this right?

She stepped forward. The floor creaked.

Everett glanced up, then did a double take. "Did, your, ah pajamas not fit?"

"I don't know." A low hum settled between the vee of her legs. Beneath her towel, she was naked. In her whole life, she'd never committed a bigger sin, yet she'd also never wanted to add to her already lengthy list of indiscretions.

"Well, shouldn't you put them on?"

For an instant, she closed her eyes, then exhaled, dropping her towel to stand before him fully exposed, fully ready for him to make her a woman.

"*Lord* . . ." He shifted his legs. "Mary Margaret, what are you—"

She crossed to him, not thinking, just doing. Acting on pure, base instinct, she straddled him, pressing her lips to his the way she'd seen in movies back when her parents had still been alive. But to her horror, instead of kissing her back, he clamped his hands around her shoulders, pushing her away.

"You have to stop," he said, "otherwise, I won't be able to."

"I don't want you to." She tried kissing him again, and this time, he not only let her, but joined her by upping her ante with a shockingly thrilling sweep of his tongue. She tentatively joined him thrust for thrust, mewing in pleasure, but then he was again pushing her away.

19

"We have to stop," Everett said. "You don't know what you're doing."

"I do." Mary Margaret needed him more than her next breath.

"How? How could you possibly know?" He released a sharp exhale. "You're a child inside. Hell, that was probably your first kiss."

"It was. But that's okay. It was perfect." She bowed her head. *You're perfect.*

"No." With his breathing ragged, he bowed his forehead to touch hers. "You deserve more. I can't just *deflower* a former nun in a shitty apartment."

"You can if I beg you to. And I am—begging. We don't know what the next five minutes will bring, let alone tomorrow. In such a short time,

Everett, you've changed *everything*. You've changed me in every possible way. Give me this last gift."

"You're sure?" Framing her cheeks with his big hands, he pushed her face back far enough for her to meet his gaze. "Because if you're not—"

She escaped his hold to kiss him.

He groaned, once again stroking her tongue, thrilling her with raw pleasurable sensation that turned her tummy topsy-turvy. When he stopped for air, he said in a ragged voice. "If we're doing this, we're at least using the bed."

"O-okay." She was beyond the point of caring.

He tenderly shifted her off of him, and then was standing, taking her hand to lead her across the room. After using the remote to mute the TV, he drew back the bedspread and top sheet before scooping her into his arms and settling her ever-so gently atop the mattress. He made her feel safe— precious—like a rare, treasured jewel.

After losing his shirt, he unbuttoned his fly. Even by the TV's flickering light, his chest was a human work of art. Chiseled with washboard abs that her curious fingers longed to touch. His pants were next to go, and when he wore only boxers, a nervous giggle escaped her. His, his—well, his penis, for lack of a fancier term, was enormous! Straining at the thin cotton fabric.

"Think this is funny?" he pointed in that general direction. "You're killing me."

"Sorry?" She laughed again, but once he joined her on the bed, there was nothing funny about the way her muscles tightened when he pressed his honed body against her soft curves. He was kissing her again, and she forgot how to breathe, to think, to do anything other than abandon herself to the sort of earthly pleasure she'd never expected.

She gasped when he cupped his hands over her aching breasts. His rough palms grazed her nipples, and then he inched lower, taking one into his mouth, laving it with his hot tongue.

Tears of indescribable pleasure sprung to her eyes.

What should she do with her hands?

"May I touch you?" she asked.

"Hell, yeah . . . Wherever you want."

She bravely skimmed her fingers along his shoulders, and then biceps. Aside from the most clinical manner, she'd never touched a man. His skin felt so good—rougher than hers, yet warm and hard where his muscles bulged.

He'd moved his kisses lower, down her abdomen to her belly button.

A wholly foreign, yet welcome humming sensation between her legs instinctively had her bucking. She felt curiously empty, as if a part of her was missing, but only Everett knew the secret to making her whole.

He'd moved between her legs, kissing her

mound.

When he urged her legs apart, she was glad for the dark so he couldn't see her blush. Surely he wasn't going to kiss her . . . *There*. Oh, yes . . . He was shocking her, thrilling her, flicking the tip of his tongue until she was crying out and losing all control. White hot light burst behind her closed eyes. What was happening? She literally couldn't breathe.

The madness began anew when Everett shifted, rising high enough to kiss her lips, while lower, he slipped his finger inside her, introducing yet another shockingly new pleasure. He tasted of her, which made this madness all the more sinful. Yet, how could anything that felt this good be wrong?

She clung to him, riding his finger, longing for an elusive something more.

"I think you're ready," he said. "But since this is your first time, I'm not going to lie—for a minute it's going to hurt. But then I promise to make everything a whole lot better. Trust me?"

Nodding, she kissed her consent.

"I'm going to grab a condom from my wallet."

A condom? The word sounded as foreign as the rest of the night had become. Of course, she knew what one was, but again, her chaste brain couldn't quite keep up with the evening's events.

He was back, hovering over her, kissing her and kissing her until she felt dizzy drunk on pleasure.

"Ready?" he asked. "It's not too late to change your mind."

"Please . . ." Desperate for him, she thrashed her head from side to side, pressing her fingertips into his back.

He entered her slow at first. There was an achy pressure, and then he plunged deeper. She cried out in pain, but then as he'd promised, Everett established a slow and easy rhythm and the pain gave way to heady pleasure. Over and over he plunged. Higher and higher together they climbed.

He kissed her and held her and made her feel deliriously happy.

Higher and higher she climbed an invisible hill, wondering, praying how she'd ever manage to summit. But then Everett stiffened and the white hot light returned and her entire body felt as if she were glowing.

"Lord . . ." he said in a raspy tone.

She was again giggling, but this time from sheer joy. "Thank you. That was beautiful."

He stroked her cheek. "You're beautiful."

He'd seemed on the verge of saying more, but didn't. Did he regret what they'd just done? The mere thought welled tears in her eyes.

"We should probably shower and then get some shut-eye."

"Probably . . ." But surely that couldn't be all? Wasn't this the time when he was supposed to hold her late into the night, whispering sweet nothings? Had she done something wrong? She'd taken, but not given. Was he disappointed?

Embarrassment consumed her, replacing her happy glow with shame.

Glad for the room's dim light, she hugged her pillow for modesty, then escaped to the privacy of a hot shower. She not only needed time to shed more than a few tears, but to process what she and Everett had shared.

With Mary Margaret ensconced in the shower, sobbing loud enough for him to hear, Everett had never felt like more of an ass.

He groaned, rubbing his face with his hands.

What have I done?

A bullet would feel better than the crushing confusion in his chest. During her impassioned speech, Mary Margaret hadn't mentioned anything that led him to believe she was looking for more than answers to her physical curiosities, but he should have known better. He *had* known better. He should have given her a chaste kiss, then lectured her on the benefits of abstinence.

Ha! Like you've ever turned down a game of blanket bingo.

But the problem he should have seen coming was that to Mary Margaret, what they'd shared had been anything but a game. To a woman who'd been a freakin' nun a mere day earlier, what they'd shared had been far more than sex. Because of his stupid speech at dinner, she'd no doubt had visions of forever. Marriage. A dog and white picket fence. Babies and Fourth of July picnics followed by fireworks over a scenic lake. She'd want the total package—she *deserved* the total package. But that wasn't anything he was qualified to give, right? At least not for a while. He'd thought she understood, but then the latest bad guy had shown up and the night had only grown more disastrous from there.

He emitted another groan, leaving the bed to find a tissue for the condom.

After settling for a paper towel from the kitchenette, Everett disposed of the physical mess, but couldn't quite wrap his head around how to best proceed with Mary Margaret. He thought the world of her. It was inconceivable how much he'd grown to admire her and enjoy her company in such a short time.

On the flip side—

The bathroom door creaked open.

She emerged, thankfully wearing chaste white cotton PJs that his associates had stashed hours earlier. Shopping for her, fingering the fabrics that would touch her skin, seemed like another lifetime.

Then, he hadn't yet gained firsthand knowledge of the fact that her supple curves felt far softer than anything manmade.

"Your turn," she said.

"Thanks."

By the time he realized now was the time to say something—anything—to make her feel better, she'd already turned off the TV and climbed into bed.

He sighed.

Took a shower.

Then spent an endless night on the sofa, wishing to somehow magically become the sort of solid, stable man she no doubt wished him to be.

20

"You look like hell," Jasper said to Everett the next morning outside the safe house. "You, on the other hand," he crooned to Baby Joe after delivering a tickle to his tummy, "look as adorable as ever."

Everett flipped his longtime friend the bird, then pulled him in for a hug, squeezing the baby between them. The past few days were seriously catching up to him. Though he'd never admit it to his angel—who now treated him like he was the devil—pretending to be normal when his life had become a complete cluster fuck was bringing him down. She hated him. God only knew how many bad guys were chasing him. And his bum knee screamed with his every move. "Good to see you, man. Things got dicey down here."

"Alone you might be lethal, but as a team . . . you know what we can do."

Everett met Jasper in a fist bump. "Dominate."

"Amen, brother." Jasper pressed his hand to the rear passenger door of a black SUV, but held off a minute on opening it. In a low whisper, he said, "Your nun's a hottie. Please tell me you're the reason she's out of uniform? Eden's about eighteen months pregnant and I'm living on fantasies."

"Get your mind out of the gutter. Mary Margaret is the real deal. Straight up angel-on-earth." Which was why Everett had insisted on getting her settled in the already running vehicle himself. He didn't want anyone else's grubby paws on her. It didn't matter that she literally hadn't spoken to him since they'd done the deed, he would still give his life for her and Baby Joe. He'd asked her what was wrong, but all he'd gotten for a reply was a shrug.

"Touchy, touchy . . ." Jasper grinned. "You remind me of Nash back when we first had the pleasure of meeting Maisey. Salty as hell, and about as much fun as a dead flashlight in a cave."

Everett shot him a look. "Let's cut the chit-chat about my personal life and get out of here. We're too exposed, and I don't believe for one second we've seen the last of Camilla Rodriguez."

Jasper popped open the door, then took the baby, settling him into a newly purchased, regulation infant safety seat. "Ma'am," he said to Mary Margaret, who sat behind Briggs, "mind looking after this one a little while longer while I make like a pretzel and squeeze into the third row?"

"Not at all." Her voice was a shadow of her former confident tone. Everett needed to know what she was thinking. Was she afraid of her new future? Or just plain filled with regret? Maybe even bored with him and their situation? "Baby Joe and I have become good friends."

What about us? The spoiled brat inside Everett wanted to ask. *Where do we stand?*

Instead, he smacked Jasper's ass as he dove headfirst into the last row of seating, then cast a faint smile in his angel's general direction before closing the door. Hopefully, they'd have time to talk on their flight.

"Safety first," Briggs said once Everett had taken his seat, but forgotten his seat belt. "Worrying about you has taken about ten years off my life. I lost count of how many times I had to reassure your sweet parents you'd eventually pop up on our radar, none the worse for wear."

"Thanks, man." He pulled the strap across his chest, then clicked it tight. "I love Mom dearly, but she's the sort who worries first and thinks rationally later. After thirty years of marriage, Dad usually follows her lead."

His angel asked, "I thought your parents were

dead?"

He glanced over his shoulder to find her scowling.

"How could you have lied about them dying?"

Shit. "Sorry. Back then, we'd only just met. I needed an *in*. You know."

Her tight-lipped expression told him, no, she didn't. As if their relations weren't already strained to the max, now this? *Give me a break.*

Briggs pulled the SUV into the already buzzing traffic, then cranked the AC. "I forgot how freaking hot it is down here. Florida's bad enough, but this pudding for air gets old real fast."

"I heard that," Jasper leaned forward, hooking his arms over the back of Mary Margaret's seat. She looked startled by his sudden appearance. "I heard you were the brains behind this mission?"

"No," she said. "I only did what anyone would have."

"Not true." Jasper smoothed Baby Joe's downy hair. "We all appreciate your help in keeping both of our boys safe."

"It was my pleasure," she said.

When Jasper earned her smile rather than him, Everett's blood boiled. This trip couldn't be over fast enough. Once they were back in the States, he'd have plenty of time to regroup. As for now? He'd have to kill time before her slit-eyed glares killed him.

Twenty minutes later, Briggs pulled up to a ragtag airfield.

Behind a leaning corrugated metal hangar sat a beautiful Seahawk MH-60, all painted pretty in jungle-camo green.

"Damn, boys," Everett shaded his eyes for a closer inspection, "you aren't foolin' around. Nice ride."

"Would you expect any less for our little prince back there and his lovely escort?" Briggs put the SUV in park, then elbowed him. "We're strapping you to the bottom."

Everett rolled his eyes. It was going to be a long day.

Mary Margaret couldn't say she'd been a fan of her first chopper ride. It was noisy, smelly, and she was still so angry with Everett that she could hardly stand to look at him.

Upon landing in Bogotá, she was thrilled to have a moment to herself in the private hangar's posh restroom. There she found white marble floors shiny enough to see her reflection, oil paintings in vibrant colors and potted hot pink orchids lining the triple sinks' crystal-studded granite counter. The opulence reminded her of Señora Camilla. Was this how she and her husband had traveled? First class all the way? It made Mary Margaret sick to think of how many people had died for their twisted pleasure.

While washing her hands, she found herself yet again in the uncomfortable position of meeting herself in a mirror. Her skin was flushed, eyes bright, short hair a rummaged-through mess. Her outfit of floral cropped pants and a silky white sleeveless blouse with matching white sandals felt like a gaudy costume, completely wrong for her plain-Jane character.

While riding through the crowded streets, to get her mind off of how much Everett's lie hurt and how little their relations had apparently meant, she'd studied other women. Their hair, clothes, and makeup. The way they carried themselves with quiet confidence, as if they enjoyed being a woman.

In many ways, Mary Margaret felt as if she'd been frozen in time, never progressing much past the twelve-year-old she'd been when her parents had been so cruelly taken. Yet in the same breath, she found herself confused by the onslaught of physical cravings and desires she'd been taught were sins, but now seemed not only natural, but needed.

In acting upon those cravings, she'd believed she and Everett would become closer, but now they felt impossibly further apart. She'd been foolish to believe a man like him would ever want an inexperienced mess like her.

A knock sounded on the restroom door. Everett called in a muffled voice, "You okay? Briggs said we're wheels up in ten."

Since joining his friends, Everett had become a different man, brimming with testosterone. Speaking a foreign language she could only assume was military slang. And then there was his lie about his parents. It hung between them like a thick burlap curtain. Rough and unwieldy. Stopping her from seeing the man she'd thought she'd known.

How would she ever again trust him?

"Mary Margaret? Please, babe. Talk to me." He'd cracked open the door, spilling his words inside not just the room, but her soul.

"You hurt me. Twice."

"I know. I'm sorry. Come out. Let's talk."

"I'm done talking. I'm exhausted. I just want to sleep for a week and wake up back in my parents' home."

He opened the door far enough to draw her into a hug and she let him.

She shouldn't have.

But she did. And against all reasonable logic, she couldn't deny the fact that standing here in his arms, she felt as if he might be her new home.

In a small, scared voice she asked, "Do you think Señora Rodriguez really has given up?"

"No clue," he said against her forehead. "Just

know that if and when she shows up again, you're in safe hands."

In that moment, she believed him.

But then he was hurrying her onto a private jet that might as well have been a rocket to Mars. Once again, she'd been thrust into a situation she couldn't control. When—if ever—would her life make sense again?

21

Jacksonville, Florida

"Why isn't briggs flying into your usual airport?" Maisey asked while not-so-patiently waiting for her baby to finally be delivered safely into her arms. Trident, Inc.'s usual hangar wasn't luxurious, but it was at least air-conditioned. This place was borderline seedy with oil stains on the pavement and holes in the uncomfortable vinyl chairs.

The stale air reeked of someone's day-old tuna sandwich.

"No clue." Arms crossed, Nash paced. "I don't like it."

"Did he give you any explanation?"

"Nope. Just told me to go with it, and that he'd explain later."

"You don't think there was a problem, do you?"

He sighed. "My guess is that with neither Joe, Everett, nor the living saint they're bringing home with them having proper entry documents, this landing isn't exactly legal. But you know Briggs. He's got friends in every high place."

Maisey frowned. "None of that makes me feel better."

"Relax." He knelt, looping his arms around her for a backwards hug. "In about ten minutes, you'll have Joe back in your arms and we're never again letting him out of our sight."

"But—"

"Stop. I know what you're going to say, and trust this—somehow, some way, Camilla Rodriguez will never bother us again."

Maisey prayed her husband was right, but then neither of them had suspected Vicente's widow of attacking the first time. Who was to say she wouldn't try again and again?

She had to be stopped.

And though Maisey hadn't told her husband, not long after their nightmarish ordeal with Vicente, she had secretly taken a concealed carry class and even had her own 9mm and ammo tucked into a secret compartment in her purse. But even that hadn't stopped Camilla's men from taking her son.

They'd been like ghosts, appearing from nowhere to take Joe, debilitate her, and then vanish.

They'd taken her peace of mind, too.

"Listen . . ." Nash walked to the hangar's open door.

The low hum of a jet approached.

Anticipation budding in her chest, Maisey joined him, slipping her arm around his waist. Finally, their son would be home. Their family would be reunited.

Nash handed her a pair of industrial noise-dampening earmuffs that he'd found on a shelf mounted to the hangar wall. He took a pair for himself, as well.

The small, sleek jet finally landed, then taxied to the hangar.

Once the pilot turned off the engine, Maisey removed her earmuffs to run toward the aircraft's already descending steps.

Briggs's massive frame filled the jet's open doorway, but upon seeing her, he smiled and moved out of her way. *Smart man.*

In the cramped cabin, anticipation tunneled Maisey's vision. She searched and saw seat backs and a table and her heart beat so loud in her ears that she feared passing out from the aching, physical need to see—to hold and kiss and cuddle—her baby boy. And then she saw him, cradled in Jasper's arms.

As fast as possible in the cramped jet, she scurried to him, and once she held him, kissing his chubby cheeks and forehead and nose, relief manifested in hot, messy tears of raw gratitude. Never had she been more thankful for her husband and the men he worked with yet again rescuing her during her darkest time of need.

Sniffing, she realized she needed to thank Everett, and the extra special woman who'd helped more than anyone else to bring Joe home. "Where are Everett and his nun?" she asked Briggs.

When her husband and his friends all exchanged worried glances, her stomach dropped.

"What's wrong?" she asked. "Are they still in danger?"

Briggs winced.

Jasper avoided her direct stare.

"Tell me," she said. "Are they at least alive? How could I ever live with myself, if they—"

"Shh . . ." Nash drew her and their son into his arms. "Everett and Mary Margaret are probably fine. In order to ensure Joe's safety, we needed a diversionary tactic. They graciously volunteered."

"They're still in Colombia?" she asked.

Briggs rubbed his forehead and sighed. "Maybe?"

22

Mary margaret fumbled with her seat belt's two halves. Her hands shook so badly, that her fingers refused to follow signals her brain was sending.

"Let me help." Everett knelt beside her.

"No, thank you. I've got it." A satisfying metallic click proved she was in control of her hands and thoughts. *Ha!* Not even close.

It unnerved her—once again being alone with him.

Her attraction for the man was palpable.

At the same time, her nerves were beyond frayed. They'd been so lucky for so long in avoiding the señora. But logic told her there was no way the deranged woman would ever allow them to leave the country with the baby, let alone their lives. That was why Briggs and Jasper had taken the baby and hidden in the back of a freight transport to another private airstrip.

That was why she and Everett had volunteered for what might very well be a suicide mission.

Everett had left a public trail of informational crumbs leading them to this place, and when the jet's engine's powered down, she knew in her heart this was the end.

The señora had found them.

"If we die," she said, clasping her hands so tightly that her nails dug into her palms. "I-I need you to know something."

"We're not dying." He ducked, peering out the craft's oval windows. His grim expression told a different story than his words.

She followed his gaze to find that their jet had been surrounded by a ring of heavily-armed men. Camilla's thugs?

"What are we going to do?" Gaze darting, breaths erratic, she searched for an escape.

"Not panic." Everett drew a handgun from the pack he'd earlier carried.

The pilot emerged from cockpit. "I never signed up for this."

Before Everett could stop him, he'd initiated the door's automated opening mechanism. A low hum raised the hatch and lowered stairs.

The man dashed for freedom, but was shot before making it outside of the hangar.

Mary Margaret screamed, covering her mouth before looking away from the mangled flesh and bone that had moments earlier been the pilot's head. His body dropped into a pool of his own blood.

Calm—no freakishly, horrifyingly unaffected—by the violence one of her men had just inflicted, the señora approached the jet in a relaxed, even sultry manner. Dressed in a figure-hugging red suit with sky-high black heels, she looked stunning. Her long hair was a tumbling fall of pure sex. Her full red lips curved into a sick smile. In physical terms, She was the very embodiment of the woman Mary Margaret assumed she would need to be in order to capture the attention of a man like Everett. The problem was that Camilla might be spectacular looking on the outside. But inside, her soul had long since turned an ugly black.

"Get in the john." Never taking his gaze from Camilla, Everett waved his gun toward the jet's cramped aft restroom.

"No." Mary Margaret raised her chin. "I won't leave you."

"Don't be stupid," Everett said. "This isn't a game!"

"You think I don't know that?" She unfastened her seat belt. "This woman—this monster—killed my parents. Who knows how many other lives she's taken. I refuse to let her hurt you, too." Not thinking, just reacting on a purely instinctive level, Mary Margaret took advantage of Everett's bad knee by standing, then wrenching the gun from his hand.

When she ran for the door, he lurched to grab her, but fell with a pained grunt. "Mary Margaret, stop! Don't be a fool!"

"Surprise." Chin raised, Mary Margaret descended the jet's three steps to approach the señora. "The baby is already safely back in his mother's arms."

"Liar." If only for a moment, the señora's confidence showed cracks. Her smile faded. Sweat marred her once-perfect make-up. "Where is my son?"

"I already told you." Hands quaking, Mary Margaret raised Everett's gun. "He's gone. Soon, you will be, too." Of course, she didn't want to take a life, but her own wishes collided with a sense of family honor. This woman had stolen *everything* Mary Margaret had ever held dear, and for that, she would pay the ultimate price.

"Mary Margaret," the señora's voice was once again smooth. "I welcomed you into my home. I've practically raised you since you were a child, and this is how you choose to repay me?"

"You killed my parents!" Her palms sweat, making her finger slide on the gun's trigger.

"That was my husband's doing. An accident.

They were in the wrong place at the wrong time. Similar to the one you and I currently share. Now, I'm tired of this cat and mouse game. Bring me my son, or I'll have my men drop you where you stand. Playtime is over. Time for the grown-ups to handle this situation."

"Interesting choice of words, Camilla." Everett stepped off the plane, planting himself in front of Mary Margaret. He held a snub-nosed machine gun similar to the type the señora's men carried.

Mary Margaret tried navigating around him. "Let me stop her. I need to avenge my parents."

"What you need is to stay safe. Yo, Raleigh! Mind taking this spitfire former nun back onto our ride?"

"My pleasure." Before she had time to launch a fresh protest, Mary Margaret was swept off of her feet and hauled into the jet's relative safety by a hulking stranger she hadn't even known was aboard.

"No! Put me down!" She pummeled him the whole way, but he didn't stop until dumping her in one of the supple leather seats.

"Chill," the stranger pinned her down. "I need to help Everett, and can't do that babysitting you."

"*Babysitting?*" Mary Margaret struggled all the harder. "Give me a gun. I'll have no problem shooting."

The man sighed, dismissing her words as if she were a pesky gnat.

SHUNNED

"Ready?" He spoke into a tiny microphone she'd just now noticed hidden beneath the cuff of his crisp, white shirt's sleeve. "We're in position." There was a brief pause, then, "Roger, that."

The jungle surrounding the desolate airstrip sprang to life.

A dizzying array of military jeeps filled with men dressed in camo from their dark boots to their painted faces surrounded the hangar's open door. Behind them, a dozen or more black SUVs rolled into position behind the Jeeps.

"Tiren sus armas!" called a voice from over a loudspeaker. *"Nosotros tenemos rodeado!"* Drop your weapons. We have you surrounded.

Mary Margaret leapt from her seat for a better view of this new—most welcome—development.

Camilla's men looked back and forth at each other.

Camilla ignored the voice and approached Everett. "What is this? Some kind of joke?"

"I assure you," he said, "the Bogotá division of the DEA is no joke. Now that they have you available for a chat, I'm guessing they'd like to keep you here for a nice, long while."

A swarm of DEA agents entered the hangar, starting the process of cuffing Camilla's men, then hauling them outside.

"Let me hold my son," Camilla begged. "Just one more time, let me breathe him in."

"No can do," Everett said. "Prison's going to be your only stop."

"*Please.*" Camilla strode closer and closer to the jet, forcing Everett to raise his weapon. "Obviously, you've won. Why not grant this defeated woman one, last request?"

"Because, Señora," Mary Margaret stood at the plane's door. "Just like you and your men took my parents from me, you took that baby from his true mother. Vicente might have been Joe's biological father, but you are nothing to—"

"Don't bring my husband into this," Camilla snapped. "He promised me a child, and I'm here to claim him. My lawyers will have me released in an hour. As long as I'm breathing, I will never stop fighting for my son."

"Then maybe you need to stop—breathing." Mary Margaret lunged for the señora, but Everett held her back.

"Whoa, whoa, *whoa* . . ." Everett held her close. "Let's keep your hands clean. "You have your whole life ahead of you. Señora Rodriguez is done. Don't ruin your beautiful future—our shared future—for scum."

"Bastard." As if life were unfolding in slow motion, Camilla dragged a long, lethal knife from a hidden side panel in her skirt, then charged for Mary Margaret. "If I can't be happy, no one will! *I'll kill you both before letting you win!*"

Mary Margaret lurched forward to save the man she'd only just now realized she couldn't live without, but there was no need.

With lightning speed, Everett aimed his weapon. The report was loud enough to make Mary Margaret's ears ring.

Señora Rodriguez fell backwards, clutching her chest, crying out in pain. Blood seeped out from under her, pooling on the concrete, in a macabre way, matching her dress. As if intending to speak, she opened her mouth, but blood bubbled from between her lips instead of words.

A wellspring of emotion turned Mary Margaret's legs to jelly. She spun toward Everett, clinging to him for support. While all around her, the hangar filled with special agents making arrests, hot, messy tears streamed down her cheeks. She'd been so afraid—not just for her herself, but Everett. How could she have continued without him when she'd only just now truly learned what it meant to live? But what if he didn't feel the same about her? What if her inexperience with men had caused her to misread everything they'd shared?

Trying to play it cool, as if she hadn't died a little inside from her fear of losing him, she asked, "What will happen to the convent, orphanage, and hospital? Without her financial support, will they be forced to close? They do so much good."

"Assuming the sisters find another supporter

with equally deep pockets—only this time around, with their money coming from a clean, traceable source—they should all be fine. Better, really."

Mary Margaret nodded. "Do you think maybe you or your friends could help me find such a person? I think I want to continue my work—never in Colombia, but maybe somewhere else where I could feel needed."

"What are you saying?" Everett's gaze narrowed. "You don't want to be with me?"

"Of course, I *want* to be with you, but I assumed now that your friends' infant is safe, our time together is done."

"Babe . . ." While DEA agents scurried around them, a low growl emitted from Everett's throat. "What I feel for you? Far from being done, it's just getting good, and only going to be better." He leaned closer and closer until planting the sweetest of kisses on her lips. The sensation was akin to flying. She loved him. She well and truly loved him. She didn't begin to understand how it had happened so fast, but it had, and she wasn't complaining.

EPILOGUE

Six months later. Chichen Itza, Mexico

"Honey, stop making those awful faces." Mary Margaret loved her brand new husband, but if he didn't allow her to take at least one great selfie for her Facebook and Twitter accounts, she just might conk him over his handsome head with her new iPhone.

She'd talked him into growing a beard, and he'd never looked more handsome.

Everett groaned. "Who was the idiot who taught you about social media?"

"You're looking right at him," she said with a laughing wink. Finally, she'd gotten the perfect shot. Now, they could head back to their Jeep rental and their Playa del Carmen hotel. Turns out honeymoon sex was the best invention *ever*!

"Don't your nursing school friends get tired of so many selfies of you and me?" he asked when climbing down from the rock she'd made him stand on in order to get the perfect backdrop of the main pyramid.

"Never," she said with a red-faced giggle. "Turns out they all think you're as hot as I do."

"Lord . . ." He arched his head back and laughed.

It was incredible how much she'd learned about her new world in such a short time. She'd aced her G.E.D. exam, then gotten herself into a great nursing program. Sure, it would be years before she earned her degree, but that was okay. In between studying, working part-time at Maisey's dress shop and helping her with Baby Joe, Mary Margaret had planned her beach wedding and now, here she was, just two days into what would no doubt be one of the best weeks of her—correction, *their*—entire lives.

Her husband's cell rang. Would she ever tire of his official title? No! *LOL*!

She was heading for a souvenir stand for a magnet to mount on their new house's fridge when she caught Everett's smile fade. Never a good sign. Usually involved work.

Jasper's wife, Eden, still complained about how

their honeymoon had been cut short by Trident, Inc. business. Surely, the same thing wasn't now happening to Everett and her?

Five minutes later, he ended the call, then tucked his phone in his pocket before heading her way with only a slight limp since, after surgery and a ton of physical therapy, his knee was almost back to normal. "Babe, I've got good news and bad. Which do you want first?"

"Do we have to leave?" She knew his job was important, but so was their honeymoon!

"Thankfully, you don't, but it looks like I might."

She groaned. "That's horrible news. What happened?"

"Remember how my friend Harding started dating that nurse? I think her name's Olivia?"

"Duh. I love Olivia. She helped me with my nursing school application. Is she okay?"

"She is, but Briggs just told me her grandparents have vanished. They're amateur treasure hunters, and were vacationing at a remote spot in Utah. They were supposed to have been home two days ago, but have apparently disappeared without a trace."

"That's horrible. But why can't Harding help find them?"

"He can—and will. But since there might be climbing involved, Briggs wants me on standby. He's already bought Maisey and Eden tickets to spend the rest of the week partying with you." The whole Trident, Inc. crew had attended their wedding, but then left. Even Everett's parents, Doris and Fred had come.

Mary Margaret still didn't fully understand why he'd lied about their fictional untimely demise, but she loved them so much, and they'd been so great about welcoming her into their family that she'd long since forgiven him.

"No." Hands on her hips, Mary Margaret shook her head. "I almost lost you once over a cliff. I'm not doing it again. Especially, now . . ."

"What's that supposed to mean?"

Not even trying to hide her pout, Mary Margaret said, "Remember how we got a little too carried away with . . . You know . . . Before the wedding?" Even though she was now a married woman, she still got embarrassed while talking out loud about S-E-X.

"Yeah . . . That was a couple months ago, right?"

"Uh huh . . . But we forgot to use protection, and . . ."

He clutched his chest, then hunched over, bracing his hands on his thighs.

"Sweetie? Are you all right?" Geesh, she was the pregnant one. Why did he look on the verge of passing out?

"Like for real? It's doctor official that we're

going to be parents?"

Teary eyed, she nodded.

He'd turned red-faced and squinty. Could he breathe?

"Well?" she asked. "What are you thinking?"

"What am I thinking?" He picked her up in a giant bear hug, but then apologized, tenderly kissing her tummy upon setting her down. "I love you. And I can't wait to raise our baby with you. And that you've seriously made me the happiest man on Earth. And that right about now, I *really* despise my boss."

Dear Reader—

If you are one of the BUNCHES of lovely fans who sent me Facebook messages and tweets and emails asking when this book would FINALLY be released, I can't apologize enough for it taking so long. In January of 2016, we started renovating our house to put on the market in April—HA! LOL!

By the last week in June, we'd finished renovations, and as I'm writing this note in December of 2016, we're THRILLED to have finally found our perfect buyers!

All of which is a long-winded way of saying that the whole house-selling process takes WAY too much time from my writing!

Fingers crossed that as soon as I'm settled into my new office, you'll get your SEAL books much faster!

Until then, I'm off to vacuum for our home appraisal . . .

Laura Marie ;-)
P.S. Keep reading for a sneak peek at EXILE!

EXILE

SEAL Team: Disavowed Book 4

1

Red Falls, Utah

Harvey "dude" Burnett's hands shook so badly that he darned near dropped his shovel. In all of his seventy-two years, he couldn't ever quite recall being this excited—well, of course the day his granddaughter Olivia had been born, but this . . . He couldn't stop smiling when giving the still mostly buried trunk's lid another satisfying thump. Even by the battery-powered lantern's dim light, he could tell they'd hit the motherlode of all treasures. "Shirley! Hurry up with that camera! We're making history, muffin!"

"I'm trying, but it's just not here. Could we have left it back at that truck stop when we went into town for the ladder?" From her perch at the mouth of the narrow cave, her voice sounded tinny. It had been three weeks since they'd loaded up their RV and driven from their home in Jacksonville, Florida to this forgotten Utah cave. Sure, he and his honey muffin had been hunting this treasure since they'd first married over fifty years ago, but this time was different. They'd actually found something, and he planned on documenting it for the whole world to see. He had to make everything just right for their History Channel documentary special.

"Nah. Keep looking." He put extra backbone into digging faster. "It's gotta be there somewhere." He'd first gotten his hands on the treasure map to a Franciscan friars' hidden hoard back when he and its owner served in the Navy. He and Jimmy couldn't have been much older than eighteen when they'd found themselves pretty near blown to hell in Vietnam.

Their field hospital cots had been side-by-side when Jimmy had opened up about the map. He'd been raised in Utah and claimed his father died looking for the treasure. Jimmy's dying request had been for Dude to find the supposed stash of stolen

Incan treasures. His entire life, Dude had periodically been coming out here, trying to make good on his long ago promise, but it wasn't until his granddaughter, Olivia, joined in on his research that things had taken a most peculiar turn.

Seems all these years, he and Shirley had been looking in the wrong spot. What they'd thought read White Falls in Navajo, *Łigaii*, had actually been *Łichíí'*—red. That discovery had led to a cornucopia of new details and characters who had all shared even more new information. Sure, some of the folks they'd met hadn't been so friendly, but with a treasure this size, he supposed that was to be expected.

Dude shoveled faster and faster until the sandy soil raised quite a dust cloud in the cramped space. He suffered through a coughing spell, but then got right back to it. The chest's entire top was almost exposed. Just a little further, and he'd be able to pry it open.

"Shirley! Where's my camera?"

"You mean this?" a man's voice asked.

Dude spun around to find a familiar figure holding not only Shirley's prized digital camera, but a gun. Poor Shirley stood in front of the man. Two more ominous figures loomed behind. Dude dropped the shovel, then slowly raised his hands. "Now, look, back in Salt Lake City, me and Shirley told you we don't want any trouble. We're amicable to share."

"See?" The man laughed. "That's where you and I differ. Because quite frankly, I've never liked sharing."

"But—" One of the men behind Shirley spoke up, only to be instantly silenced by a lone shot's roar. The gun's concussive force seemed to rock the cramped space.

The other man lunged forward and a fight ensued.

Dude grabbed Shirley's forearm, their fallen camera and the shovel, before pushing her a little deeper into the cavern.

He doubled back for the lantern.

"What're we going to do?" Shirley asked. Her dear face was dirt-smudged and her eyes were red and teary.

"Shhh . . ." They'd come to a fork. Dude veered left, but then dropped to his knees, smudging out their tracks with the shovel. "Don't you worry about a thing, honey muffin. We're going to be just fine."

A second gunshot roared.

A half-scream escaped her before she covered her mouth with her hands.

"Come on," Dude guided her deeper, always using the shovel to erase their path. "While they fight, we're going to find another way out."

"But what about the treasure?"

He stopped for a hasty kiss. "You're my true

treasure."

Dude might have reassured his wife, but inside, his heart galloped at an alarming degree. If he didn't find a way to calm down, a heart attack might kill him before these bandits got a second chance . . .

Look for EXILE's exciting conclusion in 2017!

About the Author

Laura Marie Altom is the author of over fifty novels. Her award-winning work has appeared on numerous bestseller lists and worldwide, she has over a million books in print. Laura lives in Tulsa, Oklahoma with her husband of twenty-five years. This former teacher has been blessed with boy/girl twins and a menagerie of dogs and cats. For fun, Laura's content to garden, thrift-shop or curl up with a great book.

Laura loves hearing from readers, and can be reached at the following social media outlets:

E-mail balipalm@aol.com
Website: www.lauramariealtom.com
Facebook: www.facebook.com/LauraMarieAltom
Twitter: @LauraMarieAltom
Instagram: www.instagram.com/lauramariealtom
Pinterest: www.pinterest.com/lauramariealtom